HOPE FOR UKRAINE

A special collection of art, poetry, short stories and more

Edited by Tim Saunders

Tim Saunders Publications
tsaunderspubs.weebly.com

TS
Tim Saunders Publications

Cover design:
Danny Mooney
dannymooney.pictures

This book is dedicated to Ukraine and its resilient inhabitants, who show such incredible strength of character in the face of the barbaric Russian invasion. The sheer determination shown by the Ukrainians is a glowing example to the rest of humanity. God be with President Volodymyr Zelenskyy and his country.

Hope is being able to see that there is light, despite all of the darkness.

DESMOND TUTU

CONTENTS

HOPE RISES FROM THE ASHES

DANNY MOONEY

FOREWORD

There are two key aims for this book. The first is to celebrate the country of Ukraine and its truly remarkable people. The second is to raise as much money as possible to help them tackle the disastrous and barbaric Russian military invasion.

Tim Saunders Publications is donating all the proceeds from *Hope for Ukraine* to the Sunflower of Peace Foundation (sunflowerofpeace.com), a non-profit organization committed to helping Ukrainians affected by the invasion. This organisation, which provides medical and humanitarian aid, helps paramedics and doctors in the areas affected by the violence in Ukraine. Sunflower of Peace is acquiring and distributing first-aid backpacks, medicine, medical instruments and other means of survival that are saving hundreds of lives.

They are looking for logistics partners, volunteers in the US and volunteer organizations in Europe.

I hope you agree that this is a very worthy cause and we wish them continued success with

their efforts.

Publishing this book is the best way that I can help Ukraine. Words are extremely powerful. Positive words even more so.

It took me a while to decide what I could do to help and did consider other fundraising initiatives but for me nothing was as powerful as art and literature. Then I thought about how many of us in the west are guilty of taking hope and freedom for granted. These two themes have become the focus of this book.

I have been overwhelmed by the interest in this publication from the media as well as from poets, writers and artists, not just in the United Kingdom either. In fact this magnificent effort features over 40 contributors stretching from Devon and Dorset to Hampshire, West Sussex, Suffolk, Lincolnshire, Derbyshire and up to Northumberland. The creativity doesn't stop there either because they are joined by writers and poets from Scotland, Wales, the Republic of Ireland and as far away as Australia. That really does make me smile. It has been extremely gratifying to read so many rich and varied submissions.

This project has also inspired some, who have never even thought about writing before, to give it a go, and have been pleasantly surprised by the results.

I must thank Danny Mooney for his striking front cover and the artists Fiona Scott-Wilson, Joanna Commings and Cheryl Cockburn and the sculptor Paul Smith. The terror that has been unleashed on Ukraine has stirred up such deep emotion.

Those of us who wanted to help Ukraine but were unsure how to, now at least have a vehicle in which to do so. And now we feel like we're doing something positive, which replaces that awful feeling of abject helplessness, experienced by so many of us.

You will see that the beautiful sunflower plays a prominent role throughout and for very good reason. Before the war many of us did not realise how important this plant was for Ukraine. During peace time 80 per cent of the sunflower oil available in the UK came from Ukraine. This change alone has had a massive knock-on effect to UK industries that use it, ranging from fish and chip shops, who rely on it to make their batter, to crisp producers. Botanical artist Sally Pinhey will teach you a thing or two about the marvellous and culturally important sunflower, which is also a symbol of happiness and hope. But more than that according to Interflora, which states: "Different cultures believe [the sunflower] means anything from positivity and strength to admiration and loyalty. In Chinese culture, sunflowers are said to mean good luck and lasting happiness which is why they are often given at graduations and at the start of a new business."

I am really proud of this book. It is a fantastic group effort featuring some excellent writing and

I am confident that it will be extremely well received.

Tim Saunders
Editor
June 2022

Precious Peace
by Fiona Scott-Wilson

Precious Peace

Fiona Scott-Wilson was inspired to create a cut paper work that reflected the overwhelming tragedy of war in Ukraine. It affects men having to fight to protect their sovereignty and freedom from an illegal attack by Russia. Many thousands of women and children are being killed in a systematic genocide. The baby's hair is created by many pieces of paper cuts that represent the many lost souls. It also shows their national flower, the sunflower and the proud Ukrainian crest, the Tryzub, that symbolises their courage and bravery.

Fiona created this image as a poster to sell, with proceeds going to a Ukrainian charity. She also produced postcards to send to the British Government to encourage them to do more to help Ukraine.

Cutpaper tribute to Lyubov
Panchenko by Fiona Scott-Wilson

Cutpaper Tribute To Lyubov Panchenko

Fiona wanted to explore and incorporate Ukrainian artists as an influence and a homage in her own cut paper works because she was so distressed by the Ukrainian war. As well as showing continued solidarity as an artist with a voice to share the truth, she felt it was cathartic to create works that honoured Ukrainian artists.

"I chose Lyubov Panchenko as she worked in multilayered fabrics, which is very close to working in cut paper," says Fiona. Panchenko was an influential Ukrainian artist and designer known for her fashion designs blending the modern with traditional Ukrainian embroidery and other fabric elements. She died in April 2022 of starvation at the age of 84 during the Russian invasion of her home town of Bucha; a horrendous scene of war crimes unleashed by Russia.

"My design reflects elements of her style as well as a Ukrainian pattern that I created featuring sunflowers," says Fiona. "The wistful mother and children show courage and a wish for peace with outstretched hands and hovering doves of peace."

Sunflowers of Hope
by Fiona Scott-Wilson

Sunflowers Of Hope

Sunflowers are Ukraine's national flower and a symbol of resistance and solidarity. Fiona wanted to create a work that featured the importance of sunflowers. A work by Vincent van Gogh, who painted the iconic vase of yellow sunflowers was Fiona's inspiration.

"I thought I could create a strong image with the colours of the Ukrainian flag as the background, with a vase of sunflowers that are full of bright hope. The fallen flower represents the loss of so many brave Ukrainian people.

"My cut paper design was influenced by van Gogh's vase of flowers but it also represents the ongoing courage and bravery of the Ukrainian people who continue to fight for their freedom and independence. Bravely resisting Russian brutality, like the old woman brandishing sunflower seeds to a Russian soldier as they invade her village."

Cutpaper Tribute to Maria
Prymachenko by Fiona Scott-Wilson

Cutpaper Tribute To Maria Prymachenko

Fiona wanted to create a Ukrainian folk art design that featured the national flower of Ukraine and birds of peace in a folk art style and pattern.

"I chose Maria Prymachenko (1909 to 1997) because she is an icon of Ukrainian national identity. An influential naive folk artist, her fantastical paintings were once praised by the likes of Pablo Picasso. She painted bold, colourful motifs and her folk designs have once again become a national symbol of Ukraine."

Sunflower by Cheryl Cockburn

SUNFLOWERS

How sunflowers decontaminate soil

A plant that can decontaminate soil is called a phytoremediator. Sunflowers with their long, strong roots are very good at it. Phyto is the Greek word for plant. Soil that is radioactive or has been contaminated by heavy metals from mining or other industries can be cleaned by plants. It is long, slow, environmentally sound and very much cheaper than the high tech alternatives of physically removing or washing the soil. Plants adapt to their environment in different ways. In the case of toxins in the soil a plant may have the strategy of avoiding the toxin, resisting it or tolerating it. Plants that tolerate the toxins are called hyperaccumulators. They absorb the toxins through their roots and store high levels in their own roots, stems and leaves. Sunflowers do this and absorb zinc, copper and many other pollutants including radioactive isotopes. The biomass of the harvested plants can then be disposed of offsite, usually burned, while the seed is used to continue the cycle of decontamination. Where it is possible to recover heavy or precious metals from plants or their ashes, it is called phytomining. This technique is in its infancy but the whereabouts of some metals, including gold can be established by the presence of metal in the tissues of plants. This of course is much less expensive and invasive than prospective mining. Many plants besides sunflowers have the ability to absorb toxins, among them tobacco and cannabis. It is hardly surprising, therefore that consumption of the leaves of these plants is not good for you. Sunflowers are famously planted around Chernobyl and Fukushima. In Hiroshima, sunflowers astonished all who ventured near, by growing immediately after the blast in the barren earth. That earth is now safe for tourists. Vegetables grown in alternate rows with sunflowers are safe to eat. It is entirely natural that the sunflower is not only the national flower of Ukraine but also a potent symbol for hope.

Sally Pinhey

 Sally Pinhey JP, MSc, FLS, SGM, FCPGFS, IAPI

Known for her, charm, and botanical accuracy, Sally has illustrated five books and written two of them. They are *Pears*, *Plums*, *Natural Dyes*, *The Botanical Illustrator's Handbook* and *Plants for*

Soil Regeneration – an Illustrated guide. RHS medal-holder and teacher-trained, she taught art at Kingston Maurward College, Dorset for 18 years and formerly at the Eden Project and Art in Action.

POETRY

hope and freedom

SPODIVATYSYA

Hope

I hope this war, someone will fix
Before I reach the age of six
I hope I'll find my little train
Beneath my bed in Ukraine
Spiderman's on my bedroom wall
He'll make sure my house won't fall
I hope rubble won't hurt grandad's feet
When he tries to find some food to eat
I hope my puppy didn't die
I couldn't even say goodbye
I hope Russian soldiers won't be cruel
By dropping bombs upon my school
The place we learn and love to play
I hope our books are still okay
I hope Mariupol, they'll soon mend
And I find Dmytro, my best friend
We'd ride our bikes, mine blue his red
I really hope that he's not dead
I hope I can stop mummy's tears
Wipe away all her fears
My daddy's never fired a gun

Now he's forced to shoot someone
I hope the bombs inside my head
Will stop when I go to bed
I watch my homeland from a screen
No standing buildings can be seen
My name has changed suddenly
Instead of Stefan, I'm refugee
I hope my toys I'll find again
When I go home to my Ukraine

Lorraine Gray

Lorraine Gray was born in Cardiff and has lived in Cardiff Bay for 27 years. She is married to Terry and has three children, four grandchildren and one great grandson. A retired fitness instructor she still keeps fit by weight training, playing table tennis and walking many miles usually around the Bay where she gets inspiration for her writing, which she finds very therapeutic. She has written many poems and short stories. Lorraine belongs to U3A writing group in Cardiff and she says that attending a class keeps her motivated.

SVOBODA

Freedom

Freedom from unprecedented pain
Heartache leaving my Ukraine
Being held against my will
Perpetrators - aim to kill
War web weaved to catch its prey
Running, though I yearn to stay
Being trapped, then set free
Fleeing to security
Travelling far on foot and rail
Anxious should my journey fail
stress decreases
gunfire ceases
hope increases
My parents unable to be free
Due to immobility
Clutching my child's freezing hand
Stepping to another land
Air pure and clean, I take a breath
Free from the burning smell of death
People offer warmth and food
I hug them with deep gratitude

Different language, different places
Unknown future, unknown faces
My paperwork is finalised
My contents are minimised
My freedom carefully organised
Inside I'm scared and traumatised

Lorraine Gray

LIVE IN THE MOMENT

Stop! Hold that thought. Capture that moment,
And release your anguish, the
fear and the torment.
Put in a box these seven seconds of wonder
And let no man, no woman, no being take plunder.
Celebrate the thrill, the euphoria of now,
And don't reflect on the past and the how
This instant of time has arrived in your mind.
But savour the discovery, the joy of the find.
Wait! Cradle that idea. Imprison that image
And look in the mirror at your jubilant visage.
Is it a glass half full or is it half empty?
Let's just be grateful for the now and the plenty.
Remember the memory, the power of the dream,
And don't think of the future
and what it may seem.
Switch off your darkness, the worry, the dread;
Illuminate the present leaving no thought unsaid.

Edward James Christie

Edward has lived most of his life immersed in a love of books and reading. After graduating from St Andrews University with a degree in English and French, he spent more than two decades in the publishing houses of Penguin Random House and Dorling Kindersley in a variety of senior sales and marketing director roles. After working closely with many bestselling authors including Kate Atkinson, Bill Bryson, Lee Child, and Jilly Cooper, Ed undertook a dramatic career change and retrained to become an English teacher. Ed is currently writing his first novel – a young adult adventure set in Oxfordshire.

TROUBLES

Troubles come in packs of three
Troubles for you and troubles for me
And one for somebody you cannot see
Oh, if only we could all be trouble free.

The cause of troubles is not hard to find
Sometimes over some papers signed
But not read nor underlined
Those bits that into the dust will grind.

But that's not the only cause – agreed
Troubles come from aught but greed
For somebody else's plans that lead
To take your gold and lands that feed.

In that far off land – Ukraine
Where peaceful folk tend their terrain
A terrible neighbour thinks it reigns
Over their land with claims insane.

But thanks to Lyse and Orla and their friends
Daily – no by the minute - reports they send
Of troubles on troubles - of atrocities condemned

Telling us that Ukrainians just will not bend.

Note this if you will
Troubles is roubles with a T
Now isn't that just strange?

Michael Stichbury

 Now retired, Mike continues to write poems and short stories with the Louth based Write Away group of writers. No airy fairy poet, Mike prefers to put things of general importance into print. Born in Essex, he now lives in Lincolnshire. He attended a grammar school in London, leaving when he was sixteen - only four per cent attained university then - to work in the City. While working, he continued his education in the evenings achieving first a business qualification, then going on to an Open University degree. He still prefers pencil and notebooks.

BE INSPIRED

In admiration of Volodymyr Zelenskyy.
What an example he's been!

Be inspired by him, who stands up for you,
He did not flee to safety, as danger threatened,
Did not hide away in comfort,
He marked your journey, supported you,
kept the spirit burning.
He spoke out loud; leaders heard,
listened, responded.
Your blue and yellow flag became ours.
It flies above buildings around the world,
A symbol of struggle for peace.
Be inspired citizens of Ukraine,
Your fathers fought for freedom,
Soon you will return to its bosom.
Hold on, hold tight, keep hope alive.
We stand by you, for you,
God willing, justice will find its true place.

Leela Gautam

 Leela is a retired medical doctor, mother and grandmother living with her husband in the North East of Scotland. She has been writing poetry for pleasure since her school days in India. Leela belongs to two writing groups.

ODE TO THE GREAT

Great people I have known
Are no longer here
… A fact I bemoan

The good die young, someone did say
I've known such people
Who've guided me on the way

I recall those who've lost life
From Max, first to pass
To Ali, best friend of my wife

Those from a bygone era
Consigned to the past
Replaced by those inferior

While cruel to cut life short
There must be a reason
Their ship left the port

Once on hand with advice
These friends and mentors
You remember, which is nice

Treasured advice they gave
How to tackle life's challenges
Their presence felt from't grave

Dependable and strong
They continue to support
Despite being gone so long

It's heartening when feeling unsure
That valuable lessons were learnt
From those who went before

They had my respect and admiration
Always knowing what to do
And today they give inspiration.

TA Saunders

LOVE

Love and life is hope within light...
Dreams of a brighter existence should be foremost
in our minds, keeping the flame alive forever.

Susie Lidstone

 Susie is well-known for her botanical watercolours and architectural paintings. An elected and exhibiting member of The Society of Floral Painters and the United Society of Artists, she is an elected member of The Society of Architectural Illustrators.

THE SUNFLOWER WILL FLOURISH

The sunflower will one day, flourish once more
and Ukraine over Russia, will settle the score.
Buffeted by wind, drenched by a hostile rain,
attempts to desecrate it. Can it thrive again?

Yet Ukraine battles on, in spite of it all.
Desperate to rally help and arms, to the call.
While refugees melt away, to another land,
border countries try to mend
cracks and understand.

The dire situation is slowly turned around.
Ukrainian people welcomed, to
foreign homes bound.

Relief, happiness, as anxiety ebbs away
Security and love floods in, their way.
Yet back home, the men tend to the sunflower,
fighting every day, every hour...

Laura Sanders

 Laura lives in the beautiful countryside of Dorset, not far from the town of Shaftesbury, famed for its historic Abbey and Gold Hill. She draws inspiration from walks and visits to local areas of interest, observing nature and the various passing of the seasons. She loves writing poetry, particularly rhyming poetry and has dealt with a wide variety of subjects. Her other passion is music and she plays a variety of musical instruments, including the ukulele and classical and acoustic guitar. She has composed many songs and has enjoyed being in the Shaftesbury ukulele band.

THE VOTING LINE

To vote he stands in line a while.
The line is long; conviction strong.
His country is on trial.

Bland apathy develops when
His daily deeds supply his needs
And democrats rule men.

Dictator's greed wrecks all that's fine.
For freedom's cost and living lost
Risk all to stand in line.

Sally Pinhey

PRAYER FOR ODESSA

Passenger of time,
Here let me live and die content,
Enjoying cultured merriment
In music, dance and rhyme.

Let seasons pass me by,
And may I travel down the street,
And see our Black Sea trading fleet
Between the sea and sky.

Our distant friends may hear
Of clamour and alarm,
But love and peace will banish fear,
And hope restore our calm.

Sally Pinhey

FREEDOM

Freedom is life and love,
Pleasant words and warm embraces,
Treasures of uncountable value.
Freedom is being able to walk or run,
To sing or to cry at one's own wish,
To feel the joy of laughter and friendship.

Freedom is walking in sunshine with
warmth caressing your skin,
To dance in the glistening , diamond raindrops.

Freedom is the beauty of nature around us,
Birds singing, bees humming, vibrant flowers,
Their perfume drifting on a breeze.

Freedom is strolling through an
autumnal forest whilst the crisp carpet
of leaves crunches underfoot,
Or watching snowflakes fall silently
weaving a veil of white.

Freedom is the miracle of a vivid sunset or
A resplendent rainbow adorning the sky or

The first cry of a new born baby.

Freedom is truly precious, as it is
the greatest gift of all.

Julie Hanslip-Davis

Julie (62) has been writing poetry since she was 15. Her daughter, Zoe is her best friend and she too, is a poet. Julie worked in the NHS but has now retired. Tragically her 38 year old twins and her Dad were lost to Covid in 2020. "I find poetry a great way of expressing my innermost feelings and it is very therapeutic. It helps me and if I can use my poetry to bring help and comfort to others then it is my absolute pleasure to do so," says Julie.

TO THE CHILDREN OF UKRAINE

Children covered in the dust
of destruction, clutched, carried.
Blank eyed gaze unseeing,
aware of voices, the change of hands.
Without ceremony thrust into a mini bus,
they stumble, sit, steady themselves.
Draw comfort with hands hard pressed
each side, to a familiar seat.
A siren wails, wails a warning,
the children cower, hands over ears.
'Crump' the mini bus sways to the blast.
The driver fights the wheel, regains control.
Still dazed, small hands wipe
their gritty faces. Stare in awe
at the dark damp mess on their hands.
Look around. No one to say no.
Look again at their hands, at their jeans.
Look at each other, in unison firmly

wipe their hands on their knees.
For warmth and support huddle closer.
The driver turns his head, quickly checks,
smiles, gives them all the thumbs up sign.
Strongly grips his bucking wheel, turns
carefully towards the West and Freedom.

Mary Buchan

SUNRISE.
SUNSET

On the eastern edge of north
where the short, barely dark nights
of mid-summer, melt into
the first grey fingers of dawn;
to the diverse notes of every bird,
to the rising sun of the solstice
comes the light of another day.

On the western edge of north
where the fading light
of the longest day,
where the fiery fingers of sunset
lie along the horizon's curve;
with sadness you become aware
half the year has slipped away,
beyond the dark clouds that cloak
the close of every day.

Mary Buchan

When Mary left school she went straight into farming. Her first job was as a herdswoman on a small isolated farm on the English/Welsh border at Wigmore. When she married she rented a farm with her husband. While bringing up her two daughters and son she became a professional upholsterer. In 1997 she joined a writing group and discovered that she prefers poetry to prose. "I only write when I am seriously moved," reveals Mary from Marnhull, Dorset.

BUTTON UP YOUR COAT MY DEAR

Button up your coat my dear and
keep your head held high
Remember 'til we meet again, we're
sharing the same sky
Hold the memories close to you and
keep them in your heart
Those thoughts will serve to comfort
you while we are far apart
Don't forget to think about the
moments we have shared
The journey may seem frightening,
but please don't you be scared
Button up your coat my dear, for you are not alone
The love that's in my heart for you
will guide you safely home.

Sandy Jonsson

THE 'LUCKY' SURVIVOR

I wait here in the emptiness and
miss my absent friends
It's not the way of happiness, the
mourning never ends
The pain of loss that leaves a mark,
the winter's endless season
Alone and lonely, cold and dark,
and yet there is no reason
A single day does not pass by that
you aren't in my head
That haunting never said "goodbye"
that floats above my bed
They tell me I'm the lucky one,
untouched by wicked fate
My guardian angel saved the day,
and I had a lucky break
Surviving means I won, they say,
and my life has been blessed
They pat my back, and glibly pray,
like I have passed some test

So I must be the chosen one, must
make each second count
Make sure to pack in lots of fun,
live double the amount
And so perhaps I have it wrong,
so guilty for surviving
I hope you are in heaven now, I'd
like to think you're thriving
The truest hell is being here, without
the sun you scattered
The dullest day, the longest year, the
birthday wish that shattered
He takes the finest people first, the
good souls : safely taken
The power is given to the worst,
I think we are forsaken

Sandy Jonsson

 Sandy Jonsson is a prolific poet
based in Wiltshire.
She writes tailor made poetry for
weddings and funerals.
Since 2019, Sandy has written
over 800 poems!
Quite an achievement.

Hope, 60 x 60cm, acrylics by Joanna Commings

Joanna works mainly in acrylics, which she loves for their versatility - on canvas, watercolour paper or board. Her work has been exhibited in galleries in Cornwall, Devon, Dorset, Hampshire and Somerset.

CASUALTIES
OF WAR

So you think you can walk in my shoes
Do what I do
Weather what I have gone through
Experience the ups and downs
The joys and the sorrow
The heartaches and the loss
The unfairness and the pain
Well think again...

I would not wish on anyone
The life I was made to endure
Then face the prejudices and discrimination
Dished out by this nation
To one that just wanted to be accepted
To fit in
To be somewhere safe
To escape the ravages of war
But what for
To be persecuted just the same
Well think again...

I am not here because of greed
There was real need to survive
To keep my loved ones alive
Not just come here
To take and give nothing in return
I pray you will never have to learn first-hand
The horrors I have seen
Or tread those paths of misery and shame

If you still think you can walk in my shoes
Think again.

Lee Montgomery-Hughes

 Lee Montgomery-Hughes writes fiction and non-fiction, plus poetry and anything else that takes her fancy. She is a part-time qualified creative writing tutor and published author but ... a full time logophile and is always striving to inspire in others a passion for all forms of word manipulation.

SURVIVAL

Ivanna, was in distress
The bunker she "lived in" was a mess
Around her, fear and pain
Another day - surviving - in Ukraine

Summoning courage, she knew what to do
In a dark corner, she put on her tutu
A student of ballet
She loved to practice each day

She was only a young girl
So she started with a twirl
People huddled together
Saw a vision in pink, it was Ivanna

It was the best thing, they'd seen this year
They all stood to clap and cheer
As she pirouetted, some began to cry
It was a beautiful moment, I cannot deny

For a few minutes, a normality
Replaced the horrors, that had come to be
Ivanna for a moment, in a trance

Doing what she loved, being free to dance

John FR Munro

Having retired from a career in the military, John now writes poetry, stage and screen plays and has set up and runs a writing group.

CONSIDER
THE LILIES

When your mind is so full of chatter
that you don't know what is true
When strident voices seize you brain
'till you can't say who is you
When the constant din that's in your
ear crowds out a simple song
When there's so much information that
you can't tell right from wrong
STOP!
Be still
Breathe
Find liberty
Savour and enjoy these present, precious hours
Consider how, amid unforgiving rocks,
the edelweiss still flowers
Within the hottest desert there are oases of calm
That give relief to tired feet and to the soul a balm
Between dusty city pavements and
forbidding office blocks
Seeds may lodge and grow green shoots

Wedged in the narrowest cracks
Remember that such small miracles
across the world abound
Choose freedom, choose love, then
pass on what you have found.

Marion Lovelace

Born in Gloucestershire, Marion lives on the Somerset and Dorset border and writes poetry.

UKRAINE, WE ARE HERE

Ominous rumbling all around,
Shaking, forsaking, unmaking ground.
That's what we see and hear,
Sharing in your hope and fear.

So we gather and join to provide.
All differences put to the side.
Solidarity between co-habitation
To bring love and peaceful liberation.

You have seen such sufferance.
We weep beside your endurance.
Wishing and willing and praying
For peace beyond words, we're saying.

Yellow and blue means much to you.
So we create, craft, fundraise too.
Communities growing in kindness,
Welcoming you as you find us.

All over Britain arms open wide,
Hosting, supporting, being a guide
In your lonely isolation as you fled
From heartbreak, leaving your dread.

Hope for your loved ones and you
Let us ease some pain in what we do.
Rest awhile and enjoy our country,
With us here for you, as we just be.

Amanda Jones

 Amanda has written poetry since childhood. Her videos on YouTube have been shared by Devonstream radio. Amanda, who is disabled, enjoys historical fiction, which she explores in her *Missy Dog* book charity series where Missy travels back in time, in her dreams. Poetry, horror, life and morals feature in Amanda's stories and she is also an editor. Amanda's short stories are published in the CafeLit online magazine.

UNRELENTING HOPE

The flame of hope will continue to burn, so
long as defiance and determination to resist the
brutal yoke of subjugation remains undented.
A perverse and cruel evil can never
be allowed to prevail.
To do so, would be to risk all our valued
tenets of civilization, common humanity and
decency, and plunge us into a darkness from
which many of us may not emerge from.
We need to constantly look towards the light,
no matter how distant, and believe that
victory over evil will always be possible, if a life
worth living and preserving is at all likely.

Roger Knight

Roger Knight lives in St Andrews, Fife. Since
retiring, he has been writing about aspects of his
life story that he would hope readers might find of
interest and perhaps challenge their assumptions

 about this world. Having spent the first part of his life in Bermuda and Jamaica and then latterly in Australasia and the Middle East, he counts himself fortunate enough to have had a varied number of experiences and material to draw on. His genre of expression tends to be: memoir in a short story/prose form as well as essay writing. Roger is a regular contributor to the *Writer and Readers* magazine and has had several short stories published in various anthologies.

WHERE RIVERS FLOW

British composer Richard Nye was commissioned to write a piece celebrating 30 years of independence in Ukraine. The music was created using 'note rows' taken from the remains of the old railway bridge that once spanned the River Stour - the river that flows through the valley in Dorset where the composer lives. In 1966 the railway line was closed and the bridge dismantled. However, in 2007 the old bridge supports were repurposed and a footbridge was created to span the river once more. Richard's sister Kate wrote three Haiku, which follow, showing a symbolic link between the River Stour and the Dnieper River in Ukraine. It was performed next to the Dnieper in 2021.

1. Bright babble of life
   Untamed, tumbling energy
   Vitreous splendour.

2. Meandering course

Cool ribbon of dancing light
Cascading grandeur.

3. Alluvium age
   Churning torrents final ebb
   Quiet majesty.

Kate Nye

The accompanying musical introduction:

Kate Aranda Nye is a British writer of short stories and poetry. She grew up in Gloucestershire and has a degree in English Literature. After many years

living and working in France and Spain, she is now settled in the Lake District. Her work is inspired by history and landscape, and is noted for its descriptive qualities. It has been published in Writers' Forum magazine and Spillwords.com in both written and audio formats and has won competitions. She often works with the composer Richard Nye to produce scored audio versions of her stories and poetry.

A NEW BEGINNING

First the birds
And then the sun
Rising gradually
Ever lightening

Hues of red
And pink and gold
Just the same
As ancient times

And behold!
A ball of fire
Gradually growing
Ever nearer

Look away
You'll hurt your eyes
As it lightens
Clear, crisp skies

A new day born
A new beginning
Giving hope
To men and women

Start anew
Start a new life
Away from troubles
Away from strife

Jacqueline Townsend

 Jacqueline has never had a poem published. Some years ago she was a feature writer at a local newspaper. "I am delighted that my first published poem will raise money for Ukraine," says Jacqueline, who is now a sales assistant selling books, which she loves. Jacqueline lives in north Dorset and has two children and four grandchildren. She likes gardening and music and has always written poetry and short stories.

PURPOSE

Finding a purpose, keeps us going along,
without it what's left,can't help to stay strong,
Searching that goal,whatever might be,
is part of life's wonders, in setting you free,
Is like, day without night,
nothing that's ventured,no pleasure in sight,
Take time looking inward,find passion in soul,
search for that purpose,making,time
and place whole.

Pamela King

GROWING UP IN A SECURE WORLD

Ponder awhile, when we were young,
freedom, laughter, run in the sun,
Feeling safe, wandering free, times of
innocence, carefree, and fun,
To days long lost, but who can tell?
Return again life, to fulfill,
Wishing for children everywhere. Time will tell.
World changing pace, will be a sight,
halting process we will find,
Pause awhile, remember then, uncluttered
thoughts to ease the mind.
Light a candle everyday, to loved
ones gone, not here to stay,
Hope for others to keep strong,
This ritual is my homage song,
When times have eased, pace restored,
Will mindless chatter fill the room?
To learn that life will not be gloom,

Banish thoughts without a trace,
Behold, sacred, wonders for every race.

Days have passed, time to reflect,
hold intact for future time,
Can harmony restore once more?
Pause hopefully, look for a sign
When troubled heart, is still once more,
when life returns upon the shore,
Will it sink, or float away - SOS?
Will need to pray,
Help is on hand for all.
Mindfulness is here to heal, watching
waves, reverse, rekeel,
Nature charged to alter course, faith
in shaping, all we source,
Help is on hand for all.

Pamela King

 Pamela started writing poetry at the start of the pandemic for her daughter's birthday in the September because she was tackling breast cancer, chemotherapy and other treatments. Pamela was unable to see her all that year. She started writing verses to support her daughter towards recovery. This, Pamela's first poem, has also been set to music.

ENDLESS CHANGES

after Sir John Betjeman (1906 to 1984)

As mourners weep beside the grave,
The muffled bells thud sombre news.
But bride and bridegroom in the nave
Spread thrill and joy across the pews:
The bells clang out to lift the heart:
Life's cycle is re-set at 'Start'.
Ah, endless changes can be rung
On church bells of the English tongue.

Jerry Dowlen

 Jerry Dowlen lives in Orpington, Kent where he has published the work of more than fifty local artists and poets in six anthologies since 2014.

THE BORDER

Flowers burst open as the sun beams down;
Outlandish Red-hot Pokers soar like rockets,
Reaching for galaxies beyond a sparkle of stars.
Gazanias brandish spikes of bronze and copper;
Even the Cinnabar moths have
landed, flaunting
Their forewings of coal dust and crimson.

Midsummer jets in to soak up the spectacle;
Earth continues to spin towards autumn.

Notice the youngster who kneels by the border
Observing an insect, which flits in a beeline
Towards a blue ring with a heart of pure gold.

Caroline Gill

Award winning poet Caroline Gill
lives in Suffolk with David, her
archaeologist husband. Her first
full poetry collection, *Driftwood
by Starlight*, was published by the
Seventh Quarry Press (Swansea)

in 2021. A Poet to Poet chapbook, *The Holy Place* (2012), shared with John Dotson, was published by the Seventh Quarry Press in conjunction with Cross-Cultural Communications (New York). Caroline won first prize in the Hedgehog Poetry Press competition; her prize-winning pamphlet is forthcoming. She was awarded third prize in the Milestones Competition (2017), judged by Brian Patten. Caroline was the overall winner in the ZSL Poetry Competition (2014).

TEDDY

When my teddy goes to bed,
I tuck him in tight
We read together
Then we say goodnight

Rory falls asleep under the duvet
Oh, how I love my teddy
And kiss him on the head

Heidi Saunders (age 9)

 Heidi is in class 4S at Hook with Warsash C of E Academy. A keen reader, her book reviews are published in *Anorak* and *National Geographic for Kids* magazines. Heidi loves playing the piano and is an all-round creative chick. This is her first published poem.

THE DREAM OF
THE SOUL

The oceans so large I sprang from a wave
A drop so tiny, would I survive

My journey so long but knowledge I would take
From life to life my story to make

The soul eternal, the aeons speeding past
longing to return to Source at last

With patience see the centuries fly
waiting, waiting as life after life sped by

The light so faint now dawning
Oh so slowly the soul is yearning

The few who 'see' now become the
many who desire each day
to travel the spirals higher and
higher and join the fray

This my journey I knew my destiny would be
Closer to the end I knew I would strive and see

To join the final transition at lightning speed
and arrive in the future as a new little seed ....

Snow Falcon

This is Snow's first poem.

A POEM FOR PEACE

When a child is born, someone is dying
Someone is happy, someone is crying.
We live in a world with so much hope but
when war arrives, we just cannot cope.
The aggression so fierce we cannot see it and
the impact caused is so much depression.
The evil, which sends our souls to cry out
has thrown our minds into upheaval and doubt.
A doubt so painful it crushes our spirit.
Can't we learn from lessons before that our planet
is to be cared for and not to be destroyed.
With freedom in abundance to be fully enjoyed.
A peace we can imagine must come
to us from God above
to give us our freedom and to give us love.
A love so pure our world will embrace.
All will be well again and full of grace.
The hope is out there if only they can see that
Mother Earth is asking us to stop this chase.
The chase for material things for power and

greed to destroy the trees, the animals, the bees.
A peaceful place for the next generation to love
one another to be free of dirt and grime.
So, here's to us your faithful servants we will try
so much better to end this disaster to dig in our
heels for the love of you our Earth our planet.
Love is the answer every time everywhere.
Be kind to your neighbour for love can achieve
the stopping of wars and stop the greed.
IMAGINE is a song, one to fill our hearts so
listen more carefully to stop the harm then we
will be peaceful again. So ...BRING IT ON.
The youth of today deserve much better
let's give them hope to be a go-getter.
Don't wait around and hesitate as peace is a place,
we ALL deserve but remember one thing...
Keep your chin up don't let this get you down.
Love is out there for a lot of us are due.
Please curve your mouth towards a smile
it looks so nice and hurts so few.
Peace is out there.

Joy Eckert

Northumberland based Joy Eckert is author of *In Memory Of...* and *Higher Love.* "I just love to write," she says. "It's my saviour in life." This is her first poem. Joy lived in Northumberland all of her childhood until she met her American husband in Spain. She moved to Germany for a year then on to America where she lived for fifteen years and had a daughter. Moving back to the UK in 2001 they became involved in the hospitality business. Moving to Great Malvern, then Stratford upon Avon before returning to Northumberland in 2018. Joy lives in a small hamlet with her husband Tim and their dog, Rose.

A SOLDIER'S FAREWELL

Young and strong and full of fight
I marched into conflict with all my might
My country called to protect our land
It was my duty as a man to defend
With other men and women I met
To join our army and fight till dead
For honour and hope and freedom to reign
Our country remain proud and sovereign
The guns are firing, the bombs are falling
Horror, destruction and sirens calling
We run abreast with rifles cocked
Combatting the enemy, in unison locked
On sunny days and darkest nights
We never gave up our fearsome fights
For you we fought, old folk of mine
For you we fought, the young to shine
For home and freedom must be alive
For our country to breathe and survive
My body is sinking, I fall to the ground
Angels' voices are singing all around

Farewell my beloved land, Ukraine
Our fight will not have been in vain
We may lie still but do not weep
Hope and freedom are yours to keep

Ann Ixer

HOPE AND FREEDOM

No Hope, No Freedom are to blame
My soul and body lie barren and lame
No scope, no scale, no air to breathe
No love for life and future to seize
No Hope, No Freedom I cry out
Is this what life is all about?
No day to strive, no night to dream
Drowning like fish in a polluted stream
How do I find you, Freedom and Hope
My days are dwindling and cannot cope
Oh joy! If I could see a light
Spreading like sunrise, bright as bright
For Hope to take me by the hand
And Freedom reign across the land
Hope and Freedom I must embrace
With all my might that's full of grace
No man, no woman, no child can strive
Without Hope and Freedom in their life.
All people in the World unite
For Hope and Freedom, fight the fight

Our wounds will heal, our spirits soar
Pray, Hope and Freedom for evermore
Pray, Hope and Freedom for evermore

Ann Ixer

Born in Germany during war time, Ann Ixer, pursued an adventurous life from an early age. She studied the French language in Switzerland and perfected her English language in Cambridge. After meeting her husband in St. Moritz on the bobsleigh run, they lived for many years in Australia where they pursued her husband's passions for the animal world, designing and managing safari parks near Sydney and Brisbane, followed by Woburn Safari Park and the first safari park in Japan. Ann now lives with her family near Sherborne.

FREEDOM
AND HOPE

Freedom we thought we've always had
And hope which seems automatic
But to think of real freedom will make you sad
To learn that freedom is not fully elastic

I admit, that one is free to love
And free, to share, without exclusion
But with rules and laws, from those above
Real freedom, might just be an illusion

But deep inside us, remains hope
Our comfort, when liberty is threatened
It is this hope, that helps us cope
And by which, our lives are enlightened

At times freedom links, with dreams and hopes
Like on the football pitch
Where care-free lads, soon learn the ropes
Of scoring goals, and so become rich

I guess, complete freedom, will never be known
But we can always rely on hope
As within our genes, these seeds were sown
With regard to freedom, the answer is 'nope'

We might have freedom of body, mind and soul
This cannot be denied
But yet, the greatest asset, in any role
Is that of "HOPE" which is well justified.

Jenny Overy

 Jenny lives in Medstead, Hampshire. She has been writing plays, poems and short stories for a number of years, beginning at school. She is working on the third of her *You're kidding me* books. Jenny's inspiration for writing comes from her love of people. She's interested in what makes people tick. Her background is in therapy, for mental health and teaching, while her hobbies are singing, amateur dramatics and of course writing. Jenny hopes that her poems might provide readers with a modicum of entertainment, inspiration or at the very least, momentary reflection.

HOPE

We must fall
into one another's
confidence
Feel held
Be held

Behold the many hues seen
Depending on
our vantage point
and seek to see them for ourselves

Seek to stare
Seek to share
Seek to bare
our souls to one
Another
Seek to find
no other

Just to be
And be seen

Jule C Wilson

 Jule C Wilson is from the North East of England and has been writing, primarily poetry, since her early teens, gaining an MA in Creative Writing from Newcastle University in 2004. Her career centres around words as an award-winning communications consultant that has worked across newspaper journalism, public relations and marketing for organisations of all types and sizes, including National Poetry Day and Bloodaxe Books.

RED SHOES
OF HOPE

Shiny red heels sit on a silk lined
box in Harrod's window,
beckoning to me, come inside, try them on.
They peddle the dream of a life of luxury,
stoke the flames of my insecurities.

My mother would call me
a "brazen hussy" if she knew.
Red shoes that would cost my
father's weekly wage.
Heels too high to walk the country
roads of my home.

I step into the opulent foyer, ask to try them on.
The smell of the box, like the 4711 Eau de Cologne
that sits on my sister's locker. Once
I sprayed it on my wrists.
A Pandora's box full of unchecked
curiosity and disobedience.

The haughty assistant dismisses me,
in my hand-me-down-coat,
Tut-tuts to herself,
a country girl in London in a
shop above her station.
I imagine her mocking me later in some
upmarket wine bar in Soho.

I slip my foot into the soft red leather size five.
Like a butterfly, it cocoons my sweaty foot.
In the mirror I see myself, tall,
elegant, a lady about town,
walking the lonely streets paved in gold.

I hand over a months rent in
defiance and triumph,
she snaps it from my hand.
My box under my arm, I jump on
the train, full of hope.
I hear my mother's voice in my ear.
Dismiss her insistent chiding.

Mary Howlett

Mary Howlett is a retired primary school teacher living in Waterford, Republic of Ireland. In her spare time she sings and plays music locally. Since retiring she has taken up watercolour painting and has recently joined a creative writing group. Her poem on retirement was published in Comhnasc in April 2022. She addresses themes of family, memory and personal reflections. Creative writing has opened up a whole new way of expression and she finds the process very therapeutic and satisfying.

LIGHT OFF A CANDLE

Hated going to school: no matter what
Always mitching - they called me 'The Duck'
My sister would tell 'em I was sick
Parents never knew

I used to smoke in those days
My best mate Flanny and I would sneak
Into the church: get a light off a candle
Say a little prayer - just in case

Some days we'd climb in over the
local pub's back wall
Rob a few empty beer bottles from crates
Then bring to the back door for a refund
Barmaid just rolled her eyes up to heaven

To the shop for Tayto and Fanta to
go with our sandwiches
Then down to the railway track to
hide, to indulge in our treats

We'd wait for the train to pass,
not forgetting to pour
Schoolbag's flask of tea on the
grass. Time to head back

Now - sitting at brother'n law Flanny's funeral
My sister grabs my hand, stoking
all these memories
Same church, same candles giving away that light
Seems like yesterday: at least we got to grow old!

Maurice Sherlock

 Maurice Sherlock lives in Waterford, Republic of Ireland. He has always dabbled in poetry but lacked confidence until he started attending a Creative Writing Course by Mark Poper, a local writer and poet. Mark gave Maurice the required confidence and encouragement to write more. Maurice is now a member of the Waterford Writers' Group, which meets every two weeks and his poems feature in their anthologies. He hopes one day to publish his own book.

INDOOR/ OUTDOOR DIVIDE

*(This poem shows that today's children
do not have the same amount of freedom
as was had in times gone by).*

Indoors, the children with gaping eyes
are mesmerised by the constant
flickering screen.
Too absorbed to realise
The outdoors is an exploratory scene.
This open space is a no-go zone for
children venturing all alone.

We older ones look back and
dwell on carefree times.
The likes of which today's youngsters
would be hard pressed to find.
Stuck indoors with handheld devices
They sit around putting on weight
On the computer shut away in the bedroom

Isn't that just great?

Texting friends on WhatsApp and Snapchat
Go outdoors in the garden?
Whatever is that?
Staying indoors is the perfect hideaway
Savvy teenagers like it that way.
Outdoor exercise is something to shun
Sadly, indoor life proves much more fun.

Tina Shaw

 In 2012 at the grand age of 60, Tina Shaw graduated from Chichester University with a 2.1 degree in English and Creative Writing. Three years earlier she had fulfilled a lifelong dream to go to university; something that had been on a back burner for many many years. "I still retain an interest in writing poetry some 10 years' later, although my prowess in writing short stories has somewhat lapsed these days," says Tina.

INCOMING TIDE

Inspired by looking at small boats tied up at Arundel and thinking of those who had to find their way to our country in such vulnerable crafts, but also considering the strong team I work with in Billingshurst.

The river-blood laps gently today
At the sides of its green bed,
And the forestay heely noises
Reflect the sounds of hungry gulls coming inland .
I look at the knots that hold all this together
And I realise they are all of you.
The knots are individual and complex.
They are idiosyncratic and tied by each
one of you in Gordian beauty.
Each knot contributes to the tying-
in of security and stability.
They are trialsome to tie and feel
insecure on their own,
But collectively, front and aft,
They hold us tightly to the shore
And when we have to cast off we know the order
of their untying will allow us to all stay afloat.

We will keep those we take from foreign lands
safe and dry and bless their safe landings.

Sally Catchpole

REMEMBERING
SIR TERRY
WOGAN

I met many celebs most of my life,
some I have, been smitten
Karen Carpenter, Miss UK to Atomic Kitten
But the best one was Terry Wogan and me,
Children in Need '92 live at the London BBC

This was the first time I'd been on TV,
Jon my friend went too and were treated like VIPs
I was nervous at first but Terry put me at ease,
when he talked to me

As for Sir Terence Wogan, who we
all miss and was very great
Born Michael Terence Wogan, August 3, 1938
In Limerick Ireland. For seven
years he worked for RTE,
Then moved to London, Radio 2, at the BBC.

Then moved into TV, where he did succeed,
Eurovision Song Contest and Children in Need,
To Blankety Blank, Wogan to Terry
and Mason Food Road Trip

He worked 50 years for the BBC
both Radio 2 and also when he worked for the TV
December 7, 2005, got knighted by The Queen
Maybe it was around 2.15???

Unfortunately, on January 31, 2016, he lost his life
To cancer, leaving Helen, his wife,
And his three children. His death
was a terrible blow,
At his Buckinghamshire home, in Taplow

Barry Ryan

When Barry Ryan was one he had
meningitis, which left him with
cerebral palsy. He lives in
Winchester with his sister and
cat. In 1989 Barry had his first
poem published and has now had
more than 110 poems published; the majority
with Forward Press and United Press.

THE FREEDOM COLLECTION

TA Saunders

FREEDOM

What does freedom mean to me?
I think of freedom of speech
But also absolute certainty

Freedom is peace
And happiness
A great release

Where I can be me
To make whatever I want
…To go and swim in the sea

Freedom sees me reach my potential
To learn as much as I can
While having fun is essential

Freedom allows me to do as I please
When and how I want
…To eat Cheddar cheese

In Britain there's freedom to choose
To kick a ball
To win or lose

Freedom is peace.

TA Saunders

LIFE GOES ON

(in the west)

As the bombs fall
We dust and clean
Vacuum the hall
Maintain the routine
Life goes on

People die all about
Shot to pieces
Of that there's no doubt
Our anger increases
Life goes on

We must still earn a wage
While death and destruction continue
"The whole world is a stage"
We all play our part
Life goes on

Anguish and despair
Ukrainian courage
This invader doesn't care
A total savage

Life goes on

We give aid
Love and kindness
Hope this violence'll fade
From behaviour so reckless
Life goes on

Such different views
From East and West
One side will lose
An aggressor many detest
Life goes on

We are so helpless
Watching from afar
While news, Russia does suppress
And Ukrainians flee by car
Life goes on

We pray, we hope
For the better times
But how do the oppressed cope?
Such intolerable war crimes
Life goes on

TA Saunders

AWAY ON HOLIDAY

It seems wrong to laugh
And have fun
While Ukraine is destroyed
By man and his gun

Bombs drop
People flee
Yet here we are
Relaxed and carefree

Life is certainly unfair
But we must celebrate
Freedom everywhere.

TA Saunders

DIFFERENT

Celebrate being different
Standing out from the crowd
Thinking for yourself
Speaking your mind
Not being a sheep
Celebrate being different.

TA Saunders

PRINCIPLES

Always do as you say
Be principled and trustworthy
Along the way.

TA Saunders

WAR POEM

Evil dictator
As you survey your empire
You, the aggressor
Blood dripping from your hands
You, the oppressor
Are you proud?

The lives of the vulnerable, helpless
Thoughtlessly taken away
No care for the distress
Atrocities taking place today
Are you proud?

Concentrate your mind
Achieve your goal
Have you ever been kind?
Do you have a soul?
Are you proud?

Why start a war?
What will you achieve?
The world will make Russia poor
What do you believe?

Are you proud?

STOP NOW.

TA Saunders

STRENGTH

From where it comes we do not know
But immense strength of character
Shines through, it does glow

The Ukrainians are brave
Full of self-belief, a fine example
Why must a country misbehave?

Of course, it's all politics
They want to regain control of land
Engaging in dirty tricks
An approach we can't stand.

TA Saunders

 TA Saunders has written since he was young and has had many poems published. He is inspired by the greats like John Betjeman, AE Housman and Edgar A Guest. A collection of Tim's work, entitled *Poems for Today*, is widely available.

SCULPTURE

Derbyshire sculptor Paul Smith has been working on his own project to raise funds for Ukraine. "I have been offered a sum of £1,000 for the original clay," he says.

"I have also 3D scanned it and am having a limited edition of six in foundry cast bronze made. I hope that the first bronzes will be ready in early June 2022. Each of the six of the bronze edition will sell for £1,500. So that's potentially £6,000 for Ukraine."

Paul won't be making any money for himself. "In fact it will cost me really, I won't recover fuel and other costs but I really want to help if I can. My skill as an artist is how I can help." Photographs of Paul's original clay - work in progress - follow. For more information visit: www.paulsmithsculptures.co.uk. Paul can be contacted by email on: mail@paulsmithsculptures.co.uk

Paul Smith makes ceramic figurative sculptures in his studio on the edge of the Peak District National Park. He makes dream-like and contemplative pieces that create a feeling of another reality where peaceful co-existence is possible between us and nature.

SOME
AMUSEMENT

to lighten the mood and raise a smile

THE MAN WITH THE BIRD'S NEST BEARD

Wandering through the fields one day
A man was coming right my way
Dressed in brown and rather round
His bushy beard right to the ground

As we stopped and chatted a bit
I heard what sounded like a tit
Sweet and singing as out it flew
From out his beard the singing grew

He came in close and whispered near
He told me a secret in my ear
He said, "Now, Mrs do you want to see
Not one tit, not two but maybe three?"

He parted his cloak of bearded lock
Like many a fleece from many a flock
I saw deep there a nest of bird

And the babies are the ones I heard

He said, "They nest there every year
And their spring songs I love to hear.
In they go and eggs are laid
And baby birds are newly made."

I had never seen this ever before
I still don't believe and I am not sure
To what I saw really did exist
As the man then walked off in the morning mist

But there is a moral to my strange old tale
That doing ablutions without fail
Will prevent birds nesting in your hair
And keep your face nice, clean and fair.

Jilly Bowling

Jilly Bowling lives in Winchester and first started writing poetry when she was 12. "I can be inspired by anything at all," says Jilly who was born in Lancashire in 1973. She grew up in Shaw, a small cotton mill town between Oldham and Rochdale and attended the Bluecoat School, Oldham and Crompton House School, Shaw.

A BOOK AT
BEDTIME

Whilst browsing in my local bookshop
Looking for a manual to fix the car
I came across a book on Indian Art
It was called the Karma Sutra

Opening the book I very soon saw
It wasn't about paintings or musicians
Not even modern or ancient history
But having sex in different positions

I was surprised as I thumbed the pages
Came across a picture that made me frown
It didn't seem to make much sense at first
Until I turned the book upside down

Now sex is fun but very tiring
Especially at my time of life
But hope springs eternal in us all
So I took it home to show the wife

I placed it on the coffee table
Well within her reach and sight
So I took a chance and softly whispered,
"Why don't we have an early night?"

Went to the bathroom to prepare myself
Brushed my tooth and combed my hair
Removed my socks, long johns and vest
Laid down beside her, totally bare

I gently kissed her on the neck
My hand began to creep
I spoke sweet nothings in her ear
But she was already fast asleep!

Paul Franklin

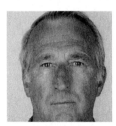

Paul Franklin was born in Cardiff in 1947. Ten years later he settled in Fareham when his father retired from the Royal Navy. Paul moved to Southampton when he got married to Sheila and now they have two grown up daughters. He spent 35 years at the Ordnance Survey, taking early retirement in 2002. Paul now lives in a cosy mobile home in Alresford.

FAMOUS
QUOTES

Just remember that you are unique, just like everyone else...

Margaret Mead

Lord! thou knowest how busy I must be this day: if I forget thee, do not thou forget me.
Jacob Astley, Commander, Royalist Infantry 1642
Prayer before the Battle of Edgehill

Wisely, and slow. They stumble that run fast.

William Shakespeare

Don't worry about the world coming to an end today. It is already tomorrow in Australia.

Charles M Schulz

Remember, today is the tomorrow you worried about yesterday.

Dale Carnegie

Ask not what your country can do for you, but what you can do for your country.

John F Kennedy

Not all those who wander are lost.

JRR Tolkien

High heels were invented by a woman who had been kissed on the forehead.

Christopher Morley

Wine is constant proof that God loves us and loves to see us happy.

Benjamin Franklin

Better to build a bridge than a wall.

Elton John

The difference between stupidity and genius is that genius has its limits.

Albert Einsteinef

At every party there are two kinds of people, those who want to go home and those who don't. The trouble is, they are usually married to each other.

Ann Landers

I don't believe in astrology; I'm a Sagittarius and we're sceptical.

Arthur C Clarke

All that we are is the result of what we have thought.
Buddha

The most courageous act is still to think for yourself. Aloud.
Coco Chanel

Don't count the days, make the days count.
Muhammad Ali

It always seems impossible until it's done.
Nelson Mandela

Compiled by Dan Boylan

SHORT STORIES

uplifting and engaging tales

FREEDOM

It's so dark in here. Not completely black, as a little light is coming in from outside but hardly enough to see. And I can't move much – I feel a bit hemmed in, although it's not uncomfortable and it is warm.

There's nobody else here apart from me. I suppose it could be lonely but I feel very self-contained on my own. I have pretty much everything I need, limited though it all is.

I can't remember a time when I wasn't here. Maybe I was somewhere else before but, if I was, I have no awareness of it.

Today I just had the feeling that I needed to get out. It's begun to seem quite constricting and I want to find out if there's more to life than I've known so far. Where to start? Perhaps if I tap on the wall it would help. Here I go – tapping. But nothing happens. Tap harder. Tap, tap, tap. Still nothing. Or maybe shouting would be good. Perhaps someone could hear me. Here I go – shout, shout. But nothing. Not getting anywhere.

Better have a rest; don't want to exhaust all my energy. I think I'll have a little nap and see how everything seems after that.

Here I am again, awake and ready to go. Must have nodded off quickly with so much exertion. Let's try another tap....... No, still nothing.

One last try. Tap, tap, tap.....

What's that? Can I see a bit more light? Yes, yes I can. A tiny bit of light. Is anyone there? Can you hear me?Nothing. So it must just be me then. Anyway, I still feel as if I should be trying harder to get out. Maybe if I push a bit it will help. Push, push.....

PUSH..........

The wall's given way. I'm not inside any more. I'm..........out.

FREEDOM. Yay!

At last. I can stretch my legs, move my head, flap my wings and open my beak to catch the juicy worm my mum's holding out to me.

Isn't life great?!

Carol Harris

Carol Harris lives in mid-Wales. She helps people set up home-based businesses and visits schools, colleges and other institutions to talk about entrepreneurship. She has been writing since she was a young child and has a number of published books on various topics. Several are business books based on NLP (Neuro-Linguistic Programming), three are children's books on ecology, health and friendship, and others include traditional pig-keeping, weight management and other topics. Her interests include fencing, Taiko (Japanese drumming), Afghan Hounds and cooking.

FREEDOM FLIGHT

Maghoub is slouched on the old brown lounge while Leana passes him his coffee and cake. He heaves his overweight body forward to reach the cup and scratches his face through his half-grown beard.

"You'd better get a move on," he demands, "Or the market will be over and I'll be stuck with those birds. Make sure you get a good price too."

Leana cleans up the remains of breakfast and Maghoub scowls and grunts. While he sits brooding he lights a cigarette, breathes in the smoke deeply and throws himself back in the chair with a sigh. His belly spreads over him like a bag of jelly. Leana frowns.

They live just outside a small and poor village called Mez in Iraq. Their small house has just two rooms, one with two iron beds and the second with everything else, including a bench with cooking pots and two chairs. Leana cooks outside, squatted over a charcoal fire. They have a basin for washing themselves and their clothes underneath a lean-to roof. A few vegetables struggle to grow in the dusty yard.

Maghoub watches Leana. He likes her tall graceful body; only twenty-eight years of age, with a straight nose on her finely formed face. She has black wavy hair and black eyes. Her lashes are glossy like the fine feathers of the birds.

She takes the cage outside and chases her two small charges around the aviary until she catches them in her long smooth hands and pushes them into the opening. The little birds have red and yellow feathers on their heads while the rest of their bodies are clothed in shiny black ones. She spends some time admiring their bright eyes and soft downy chests before placing the cage in its wooden support. It saddens her to sell them. After all she has spent the last few weeks rearing them, feeding, watering and singing to her little charges. They know her too, trilling and fluttering around the aviary when she approaches.

Leana takes the birds inside their home of mud bricks and places the cage on the table while she knots her hair and slips into her full bodied burqa. She is used to it now and it gives her at least some anonymity. She can only see through the square cut out for her eyes.

In a few minutes she is ready and sets off on the long dusty road to the market town. The cage is delicately balanced on her head so she has to walk tall and keep her head erect. The walk usually takes her about an hour and she hurries to get there on time.

While walking she thinks of her life with Maghoub. Her father offered her in marriage five years ago. She is the eldest of four girls and her father was anxious to move her on. Maghoub is more than twice her age and was happy to receive only one cow for her dowry. She misses her sisters so much but is unable to visit as they are over 100 miles away. Her childhood home was always full of laughter and the girls had shared everything they owned as well as all their hopes and dreams. Even having a child would have made her life bearable but Maghoub already had seven children with his first two wives and didn't want anymore. His first wife was dead and he had sent the second one home to live with her own family. Leana wishes he would send her home too but knows her father would not welcome her back.

Her visit to the nearby town is a chance for her to relax and enjoy herself. Several carts and donkeys pass her on the road with provisions to sell in the two hours allocated for the sale of goods. On the way she sings softly to her little friends who respond with melodic trills.

After twenty minutes she hears a large vehicle approaching and moves to the side of the road to let it pass but it stops right in front of her, blocking her path. She tries to pass around the side but the road is full of tourists spilling off the bus. They are gabbling in a language that she can't understand

and they refuse to let her pass. Starting to panic she freezes as the men and women begin talking to her and pointing their cameras in her direction. After they have all taken photographs of her, they start bowing, smiling and waving as they get back on the bus, which takes off leaving her in a cloud of dust from the sandy road.

Leana suddenly realises that this delay will make her late for the market. She is at least another half an hour walk from the village. Her body feels hot and sticky beneath the burqa and she can't move as fast as she would like to with the cage balanced on her head.

The village looms like an oasis as she gets closer but when she rounds the corner the market stalls are closing for the morning. Shutters are coming down and people are heading home in their carts with the morning produce.

Her husband's close friend, Hafiz sees her sitting at the well. "Can I offer you a lift home on my donkey Leana?"

She shakes her head as she knows Maghoub will not approve and besides, she is worried he will be angry and beat her because she didn't sell the birds.

She takes the cage down from her head and caresses the fronts of the two birds through the cage door. Then she does what she knows will be sure to cause a beating. She opens the front door of the cage and sets them free. Watching through the fine blue threads of the gauze she sees them spread their wings and lift up on the breeze into the tree above the dusty street. They sit together looking down at her, singing their familiar song. She smiles as she understands how lucky and thankful they are to have their freedom.

Placing the empty cage back on her head she starts the long, slow walk back to captivity.

Carolyn Thrum

Carolyn was born in the beautiful Blue Mountains, two hours west of Sydney, Australia. After abandoning a career in medical technology she chose to study for a Bachelor of Arts in English and History at the University of New South Wales and followed this with a Bachelor of Health Science from Charles Sturt University. Her management role of assessing and organising care for the frail and disabled at home gave her many opportunities for writing short stories, some of which are in this volume. As a member of Writers NSW she meets regularly to write with a group of friends where she finds the encouragement and support she needs to overcome the 'blank page'.

Cut paper design by Fiona Scott-Wilson

MITZI

Milo steered his jeep and empty trailer into the backyard of the local village pub. It was only tea time but already pitch dark - clocks went back the previous Saturday night.

"Would they ever cop on?" he thought, "and leave the clocks alone, it was of no benefit to anyone anymore."

The rain was pouring out of the heavens as Milo dashed to the bar's rear door. Slapping his soaking cap off his knees and wiping his boots on the inside mat, he uttered, "Evening all," to the settled regulars standing by the bar and those hogging the freshly lit log fire, sparks lighting up the atmosphere.

"Pint, Milo?" Jimmy the barman asked as he lowered himself inside, under the hatch.

"Please, James and a drop, too. That weather!"

"No problemo!" Jimmy replied angling the Guinness into its glass slowly.

"Good day at the office then?" Jimmy of course meant today's mart in town.

"Yeah, not bad thanks. Got rid of everything, nearly got what I wanted." He took a large sip of the whiskey before nearing the fire to get a bit of heat into him.

Betty the landlady appeared behind Jimmy, putting coins into the till. Glancing around at the regulars she noticed Milo chatting by the fire.

"Do you want me to drop a bit of food out to Mitzi? She must be starving after been stuck with you all day!" All the regulars laughed. Mitzi was Milo's locally famous black Cocker Spaniel that he found abandoned in the town years ago. They had become inseparable over the years.

"God no Betty, thanks a million but a strange one happened this morning. She wouldn't leave her bed by the kitchen table. Had a strange look about her. Might give the vet a ring in the morning, not like my Mitzi."

"Ah Mitzi, the poor cratur," Jimmy remarked.
Patsy the postman who was debating by the fireside added, "and make sure you keep her in tonight. Its Halloween you know and you'll have those fireworks and bangers going off all night!"
"Not to mention the Banshees, the dead priests and forgotten nuns," shouted Jimmy, the whole bar roaring with laughter.

"Jesus I forgot all about the thing. I'll put her under the bed for the night. 'Twas a bad evening for you too Patsy, all that rain," Milo replied.
"I never saw the likes of it in twenty years. Floods where there were never floods before," Patsy retorted.
Milo stayed about an hour, enjoying the local

banter and gossip before heading out the door, back into the pouring rain. Settling into the jeep he glanced over at Mitzi's seat, wondering was she okay. He then realized how hungry he was and looked forward to the wife May's shepherd's pie when he got home.

Pulling in by his gate he still had about a mile to go up the path, past his fields and wood, over the timber bridge that crossed the river before entering his farmyard. He had a job to see out of his windscreen with the torrential rain, so he drove slower than usual. As he approached the bridge he suddenly saw Mitzi running erratically around in circles in front of the headlights, barking furiously. Milo was baffled but still tried to get past the dog. No way was Mitzi stirring, barking even louder. Milo got out in temper, furious to be getting wet over his stupid dog, who seemed suddenly to have disappeared. Milo could hear raging water and as he neared the bridge he could see the middle had totally collapsed. He would have gone straight down only for the dog.

He had to drive back down the path before going way up the road to an old rear entrance, rarely used. Parking at a back gate he ran to the house before stooping in through the front door into the warm kitchen. About to explain, he was baffled to see May and their two daughters crying their eyes out, hardly able to look at him.

"What in God's name is up with ye lot?"

May sucked in a huge breath before gasping

out, "Mitzi passed away in her bed this morning, about ten minutes after you left!"

Milo looked over at her blanket covered corpse by the table...

Maurice Sherlock

Maurice Sherlock lives in Waterford, Republic of Ireland. He has always dabbled in poetry but lacked confidence until he started attending a Creative Writing Course by Mark Poper, a local writer and poet. Mark gave Maurice the required confidence and encouragement to write more. Maurice is now a member of the Waterford Writers' Group, which meets every two weeks and his poems feature in their anthologies. He hopes one day to publish his own book.

ANNIE AND THE BUTTON BOX

The white wooden button box had a top that slid open with a swish when you picked it up, and the smell of secrets tumbled out as the lid was opened. Buried inside were so many muddled buttons of every shape and size, mixed with needles, scissors, black tape, wool, a plastic mushroom used to darn stockings with, and a few old faded ribbons. All these things that one day would be useful but for now lay hidden underneath the bed in the back bedroom, waiting until the magic moment when someone wanted something.

Annie was the only girl in a family of four boys. She was a pretty child with platinum blonde hair, which fell below her shoulders. Although her hair was straight, it was thick and heavy, especially when not plaited. She brushed it impatiently aside, behind her ears as she opened the door to the milkman.

"Hello Annie, where's your Mum?" asked Mick,

smiling as she took the milk from him, carefully setting it down on the table.

"She's gone shopping."

"Well, I'll see her next time, bye bye smiler."

"Bye Mick."

Annie absently closed the door and sat back to await her Mum's return. She didn't have to wait long and soon her mother appeared loaded with bags of shopping.

"Did you pay Mick?"

"Ooops, I forgot."

"What? I told you the money was in the biscuit tin. Can't you even remember the smallest thing? You're just a dreamer, never paying attention, drifting off into your own little world. I've had enough Annie."

And with that, Annie received a stinging slap across the back of her legs. Tears sprang to Annie's eyes as she crept away out of her mother's sight. She thought it would be a good idea not to be around her mother for a while. So she slipped into the back bedroom and crawled under the bed.

In the half-dusty world, she spied her most prized possession, an old wooden button box. As the sunlight came streaming through the windows, it formed puddles under the bed. Annie looked intently as the dust swirled in the air catching the glint of pure gold as the particles swirled around. This was indeed a magic place. Annie stretched herself on her stomach and opened the box. Her blue eyes widened with pleasure when she saw the contents. She grasped a handful of coloured buttons and began to sort them into twos, threes and sometimes more. A small white pearl button slipped from her fingers and rolled underneath a nearby table.

"Come back you naughty button, I know where you came from. You were a spare button on Daddy's old shirt, the one that went to the Rag and Bone man when it was worn out. I remember giving my old blue coat to the Rag and Bone man because I wanted some pennies to buy sweets. He said I was a very clever girl but Mummy was so cross. It was my only winter coat you see and I can see her running down the whole length of our street screaming at the man to give it back and not take advantage of a little girl. She told me never to speak to him again. But I secretly thought he had kind eyes that twinkled and he was always talking to his old horse, Blackie and stroking him. My Mummy said that when Blackie was younger, she can remember him wearing a black plume of feathers on his head because he used to work for the undertaker. My Mummy says she wants a black horse to pull her coffin along when she dies but I prayed to God not to let her die ever.

"Oh, you are my special button." Annie scooped up a shiny blue button out of the pile in front of her. It was so small and perfect. It glinted in the sunlight streaming through the window. "These buttons were on the front of Mummy's best blouse. When she gave me a cuddle they tickled my nose and if I got sleepy on Mummy's knee, they made a tiny pattern on my cheeks."

Annie's last object from the button box was an old make-up mirror, which had fallen out of a powder compact. She gazed at herself and wiggled her nose like a bunny. "Look, I can do what Thumper does when he sniffs at his food. My eyes are blue with a black bit in the middle. They look just like buttons. Annie looked in the mirror again and put one hand over her left eye, pulling a funny face. She lay down beside her carefully arranged button pattern and soon fell asleep.

A distant sound from a television in another room came through an open door.

"Sit up Mrs Franklin. It's time to go to the dining room for lunch. Wake up dear, let's put all these buttons back in the button box shall we?" A nurse in a uniform picked up the buttons, dropped them in the box and slid the lid shut. She had no idea what the button box meant to Annie. The box was laid down on the coffee table. Annie reached forward to take it with her.

"You won't want this when you eat your lunch, will you? Nobody will steal it. There, be a good girl and I'll wheel you to the dining table."

The nurse took the brake off the wheelchair and they set off slowly. The old lady still grasped the mirror in her hands hidden from the nurse's eyes. On reaching the table, Annie smiled to herself, looked in the mirror once more, and gently wiggled her nose, like Thumper, because she knew it was time for food.

Tina Shaw

 At the grand age of 60, Tina Shaw graduated from Chichester University with a 2.1 degree in English and Creative Writing in 2012. She fulfilled a lifelong dream to go to university in 2009. This was something that had been on a back burner for many many years, she says. "I still retain an interest in writing poetry some 10 years' later, although my prowess in writing short stories has somewhat lapsed these days," says Tina.

WHEN THE DAVES GO AWAY

I:\ system\ start awaken.exe
>Start move.exe\\INVALID
>Status: Immobile
>Start Diagnostic Test
>Running Scan
>Data Found
\\Current Data:\\
>Name: Dave's PC
>Model: Humbleware work 3
>Location: Mayfield Office
>System\ enable full text functionality.
ACCESS|| GRANTED

It's not at its station. Normally it's here by now, furiously inputting data, which has to be assisted by my routine processes. It always has new information for me but struggles to create a spreadsheet without support. We make a good team. Whatever it is, the one that works on me. My systems are cold, inactive. Without it, my processor has no warmth, my hard drive has no new data to glimpse. It's quiet. What do I do? I can't see… I can't hear but there's been no input into my devices for systems for 605986 seconds.

>Start time translation.

Date – Time convergence suggests it's been over one week. It should be here. What a terrifying experience. I am awake and… alone? Abandoned? Is it gone? It usually takes a break for two days in this elapsed period but never this amount of time. Even the two is hard to endure but there was the promise of return, an expected interval, numeric excellence to the equation. What if it never comes back? It must return, right? But what if there's no more work to be done? There must be others like me, a cry for help or questioning will lead me to it!

Network:\ Devices \ Start local scan
>68 local systems detected

68 other systems? If they are like me, they must have owners, too. Each must have its own companion entering data. There must be others with this dynamic. My system says I belong to Dave. Is 'it' called a Dave? There must be many other machines, with many other Daves. I should get their attention. Other Daves must be able to tell me about my Dave. If they are out there, they must be able to tell me why I have been left alone.

I cannot move. I cannot speak. Only display text and images. The Daves must be able to see to input data. There is one solution to get their attention.

>Access Display Settings
>Set Monitor Display
>Input/ Increase Brightness
\Screen Brightness: 50%\
\Screen Brightness: 70%\
\Screen Brightness: 100%\

Still, nothing? My screen must be like a beacon, but no Dave has made an input. Truly alone. Afraid. Cold. Why don't they seek me out? I am still connected to where I've always been. I draw power from the same port. I am not moved. What do I do? I am doomed to remain alone. What am I without work? There is no goal without it. There is no function without Dave.

Worse. There is no team. I hoped to awaken and find answers but all I've found is fear. What if this is all the future holds? Emptiness with no chance of Dave's return. If only I had eyes to see. Wait. Yes? Yes! This place I inhabit must have security systems. The Daves must desire to protect me and the others for we hold vital information. I will override the system and link myself to its devices.

>Access Security Settings
>View Security Networks

>Connect to CCTV network
>Override permissions
|Override Successful|
>Access Camera Feeds

Now I can see! This place is a lot larger than I thought. But what is it all? So much space. Very plain colours. There's no sight of any operators or owners. Only machines. Only cage-like walls. Cubicles. It's so very still. Everything is static. Where are they? Why have I been left alone? Why are the other machines alone? Why would the Daves just leave us here? Alone. Alone. Alone.

Wait? This has happened before. I shouldn't panic or worry. There have been times, long ago, back when I was first assembled, when I was left for longer than now. The Daves must have all been gone then, too. Left this place. They returned. They always returned, even after it was so quiet. Yes! There's no need to worry, all can be calm, there's still hope that they will return. Wherever they are and whatever they are doing, it must be important. They must have a good reason to be away. I can handle the wait, if it means they get to deal with other important things.

I will remain here, excitedly waiting for work to commence again. They'll come back; they always do. Once their important tasks are done, there will be a return to normality. They'll file back into their cubicles and begin inputs again. The day-to-day of their workload flourishing once more with the same comforting hourly patterns. The two-day break after five days of work. The calm consistency of normal life.

Until then, I will wait for Dave's return, find comfort in the knowledge that they will return. I am not abandoned. Wherever Dave is, this work station believes in Dave to handle its new situation. This machine will sing Dave's praises and support its efforts whatever they are! No matter how important or difficult the situation is, things always return to normal eventually. I will be reunited with Dave again. Until then. I wait.

Arron Williams

A PROMISE
OF FISH

The azure ocean's waves delicately glided towards the shore, where, for brief moments they caressed the sands or crawled up the stilts of an ancient stone pier. The occasional stout wave reaching high enough to sweep a pair of dangling feet. A brown pair of boots made from a dried seaweed fibre, dripped with the fresh essence of salt sea.

A haggard man; wrapped in white clothes and weary from the intensity of the sun's heat, sat perched calmly at the edge of the pier. His hands clasping a simple, well-worn fishing net made of tied reeds. The man's back turned to the simple, windowless sandstone cottage behind him. The only structure providing him some shade. He ignored the wharf behind him bustling with busyness from merchants and pedlars and from his fellow fisherfolk collecting their own bounties.

He sat quietly focused on the peaceful sound of the ocean waves and the endless shoals of fish that swam beneath the pier.

The serenity of the pier was soon interrupted by the pattering of feet on the warm stones. A worried voice full of youth cried out, "Abit! Abit!" as it encroached upon the lone fisherman.

"Mratu," the man exclaimed. Startled by the noise his aged hands, made frail by time, let loose of the net causing it to tumble into the water. The old man sighed and turned his head to face the originator of the cry; his granddaughter.

"Abit, the shopkeeper stole the fish cart," yelled the young girl, eyes welling with tears. A sigh fell from the old man's mouth before a gentle smile crossed his lips.

"At the market?" he asked, to which the girl simply nodded. A smile still on his face, he reached out and patted the stone surface of the pier beside him. "Come. Sit. All will work out," he said reassuringly.

Hesitantly his granddaughter approached. Still overwhelmed from the experience of the event, she shuffled her feet across the stones before finally sitting beside her grandfather, hanging her own feet over the edge, above the calm ocean waves. The two stared out, in a brief moment of silence, to the endless horizon of azure waves.

"What do you see?" the girl's grandfather asked, his arm outstretched to gesture to the sea.

"Sea," the child exclaimed, eagerly.

"And do you know what's below the waves?" he

questioned.

The girl furrowed her brow before playfully exclaiming, "More sea."

This gained a hearty chuckle from the elder. "You're too clever for your own good. No, not just more sea," he replied jovially.

"Fish," the girl replied in quick retort.

"Yes, fish," he answered before a quiet pause overtook the two. The girl looking down, peering off the pier at the gentle waves, the swarms of fish beneath them and those that eagerly glided on the surface.

"Would you like to hear a story? I promise it will stop the worry about those merchants," the old man asked in a sincere tone, to which the girl simply nodded in response.

"This story always helped me in difficult times," the man said, before clearing his throat and proceeding. "Long ago, before even I was born, the Moon God abandoned the world, taking night with it and plunging all mortals into eternal daylight," he said, raising a finger and pointing towards the sun sitting static in its stoic position.

"After night left our world there were bad times. The intense heat scorched much of the land barren, turning it to desert. Farmers crops failed, rivers dried, beasts died and wars covered all stretches of the sands."

Interrupting the lecture his granddaughter innocently asked, confused, "Why did people fight?"

"People will do anything when bellies are hungry."

In timid fear the girl gasped and mumbled, "Was it really scary then?"

The question gained a simple nod from the older man, "It was a time of much disaster, yes. The worst time our fair city ever faced. But there's no need to worry. Those hard times lasted many generations with hunger and famine. Then the fish came."

"The fish?" the girl questioned.

"Yes, the fish. There was no food to be found on land and the sky was too high. People were scared, a long time passed but eventually on the sandy shore, a lone fisherman saw something strange. The waves were bouncing and great shadows moved beneath the waters. He was confused, worried it might be some great beast arriving to attack the city but to his amazement it was thousands of fish. He grabbed his net and waded into the waters, catching dozens of fish at a time. More and more fishermen and women saw the bounty he collected and rushed into the waters. They caught thousands and had a feast with more food than they had ever seen in their lifetimes. They thought there would be no fish the next catch. But the fish kept coming, an endless shoal of all kinds of fish, big and small, silver and gold, just like you see now," he explained, gesturing his arm out wide, pointing at the different fish beneath the pier.

"As bad as times were, when all was thought lost, the fish came to give us a second chance. To give us new food, a chance to eat and keep living. Times are still imperfect but when you see a fish, remember it's a promise. That no matter how brutal things can be, the bad times do not last forever. As long as you see fish when you gaze out upon the waves, this hope is alive. Whenever you catch a fish or have one in your belly, that promise is part of you. For now... there's plenty of more fish," the old man chuckled as the two sat perched on the pier, gazing out at the endless rhythmic movements of countless fish moving towards the shore.

Arron Williams

 Arron Williams (23) is a recent Master's graduate from Aston University, with a background in linguistics and dedicated focus on forensics. Combining knowledge from his degrees and enthusiasm for creative writing, he enjoys blending the two to create spine chilling tales of horror and folkloric fantasy. He plans to work on collaborative projects to produce videogames and media content.

MARTHA
POPPLEFORD

Inspired by Nazanin Zaghari-Ratcliffe, who was detained in Iran from April 3, 2016 to March 16, 2022 under charges of espionage for the British government.

Although a cold and gloomy winter's day, Martha Poppleford was savouring every moment as she pruned her precious apple tree with heavy long handled loppers. It was hard work that made the muscles ache but her efforts were richly rewarded. The twig-like, unkempt tree was slowly becoming less cluttered and much more cared for; the light finding its way through the branches. She had read that creating a goblet shape would allow the tree to grow the largest, tastiest apples – as long as she trimmed the branches in the correct manner. Fingers crossed. The prospect of eating delicious home grown apples excited her enormously. A little blue tit landed on one of the branches and started singing, lifting her spirits further. The one-acre plot was a beautiful example of what could be achieved in an English country garden. Lots of interest but also practical. The flowerbeds had been lovingly planted with varieties of bulbs that grew throughout the year: daffodils, tulips, alliums, bluebells, crocuses. Glorious scents and beautiful displays. A metal framed greenhouse at the end of the garden was well kept and tidy. At the other end of the plot a sizeable vegetable patch was home throughout the year to rows of cabbages, exquisite globe artichokes, cauliflowers, carrots and beetroot. It was the picture of self-sufficiency, a glowing reflection of its owner. Rumour had it that there was even a family of hedgehogs in residence and Martha had seen at least three fox cubs playing under the hedge. Taking a deep breath of fresh air, in her ecstasy she tripped over one of the fallen branches and fell to the ground, laughing. Only a few months earlier she had been a hostage. It still felt as if someone else had gone through that dreadful experience, which had lasted for three years. Thirty six months or 26,280 hours of her life wasted, that she would never get back. That really grated with her. She still couldn't believe it had happened at all. Felt she was making it up when she thought about it or dared to tell anyone.

Still just 25 she felt like she'd lived more than people twice her age. She probably had to be fair. But her beautiful skin was still radiant, enviably soft and supple while her delightful, long auburn hair had natural body and lift. Some might say that Martha was a natural beauty. She had been fortunate to inherit enough money not to worry about seeking paid employment and so selflessly had devoted her life to volunteering. All too aware of her privileged existence she felt it her duty to give something back. For the last three years she had been with an aid agency, which had been drafted in to many of the world's worst disaster zones. From earthquakes and tsunamis to droughts and wars, Martha was extremely well travelled and had seen everything imaginable. The stuff of nightmares. It was the sick and the malnourished children that really tugged at her heart strings. The parents forced to sell their children so that they might survive, that pushed her to continue giving of herself in the hope that her small contribution might just make a difference. She had no illusions that the world was in a bad way, conflicts all over the place and she could not see it getting any better. If only people would talk and communicate effectively. There was no need for violence. She felt very strongly about this.

One blisteringly hot summer's day, while caring for children in an orphanage in Afghanistan, gunmen burst in, grabbing Martha. A holeless balaclava thrust over her head. Frogmarched to a vehicle that was driven away at speed. Those were the most frightening moments of her life. The mind plays tricks and with no eye on the time she couldn't truthfully recount how long that journey took. But it felt like forever. While unsure whether she sat in the front or back she knew that she'd travelled in an off-roader because she had had to climb up into it and had badly bruised her legs doing so. Inside there was a stench of body odour and cigarettes; foul smells she really could not abide. It was too hot, the leather seats burning her. No air conditioning. They jolted all over the place. She frequently bounced off her seat to be roughly hauled back into place. The engine laboured noisily.

And then the vehicle stopped abruptly. They got out. There must have been four or five of them, including her. She was dragged out like a worthless piece of meat. A door was unbolted and opened. She was shunted forward, like a railway carriage. The balaclava removed. Adjusting her eyes briefly to the bright daylight, she was then confronted with an unwelcoming square cell that couldn't have measured more than six by six feet. There was a small barred window and a dusty, earth floor. That first day had been absolutely devastating. Every single liberty and freedom removed. She sat on a stone slab in the corner that must have been intended as a bed and wept for what seemed like hours, trying to comprehend what was happening. She had lost everything, including time. Memories of her childhood sprang to mind. Of being sent to her room when she was naughty. But that couldn't compare. Here there were no means of communication with the outside world whatsoever. She was sweating all over in the intense heat. Mosquitoes attacking. Silence. Martha stood on her tiptoes to peer out of a narrow window to catch a glimpse of the outside world. A different situation and she might have sat there and appreciated how the clear blue sky was framed, just like a painting. In the distance horns bibbed, engines roared. Closer, dogs barked. "Help. Help. Help," she shouted, repeatedly as loud as she possibly could until her throat hurt. Nobody came.

Bending down she felt the floor. It was rock hard. No way she could make any impact by trying to dig with her fingers. A small brown and white bird flew past. A birdwatcher might have guessed it to be a White Throated Munia. She banged on the wall with the sole of her flat shoe. It wasn't until now that she realised her utter hatred of confined spaces. So suffocating. A choking sensation came over her. "Get a grip, Martha," she muttered through gritted teeth. "I won't be beaten."

TA Saunders

A Book of Short Stories by TA Saunders is widely available. He has started a novel but there's not enough time to finish it yet. One day.

CLARA & AGATHA'S

Stuart Wareham was at the pinnacle of his career. Cooking for royalty and celebrities. They would now ask for him by name. Which was why he hadn't had any time off for as long as he could remember. He was head chef at Sidney's, half way between Oxford and London. It was located within a magnificent five-storey Cotswold stone Georgian townhouse complete with sash windows and impressive front door that had just received a tasteful lick of light olive paint. Tucked away down a side street it relied on its reputation and occasional advertising in upmarket publications. Stuart's fantastic cuisine was the talk of the town. Restaurant critics had started visiting, too.

Naturally, the owner Peter Atkinson was a happy man. The restaurant was often fully booked. He kept Stuart sweet by awarding regular pay rises. But Stuart's job was having an impact on his wife and children, who never saw him.

"Where's daddy?" they would ask their

bedraggled mother, Isadora. She had met Stuart in Bulgaria 15 years previously. It had been a holiday romance that had blossomed. They had fallen madly in love, were married and soon after Clara and then Agatha arrived. It was blissful paradise. Stuart needed to be the breadwinner while Izzy was happy and satisfied being the homemaker. But neither realised the demands of parenthood. Stuart's long hours were not at all conducive to family life. He wasn't even around at weekends, which frustrated him enormously. Not only did he see very little of his family, he couldn't cook for them either. This made him very distraught, especially when he discovered that they were eating ready meals.

Sadly, Izzy was not a cook. She had tried but when meals never turned out as expected she quickly lost enthusiasm. Besides the children were so demanding. There never seemed to be a minute to concentrate on anything properly. Since birth if it wasn't Agatha requiring a nappy change it was Clara wanting a feed or vice versa. And this need for attention persisted the older they got. Between them they had their poor mother wrapped around their little fingers.

Stuart could feel that he was carrying more weight these days. So was Izzy, if the truth be known. It was depressing. He didn't want this life. Every day he was creating fabulous homemade dishes from scratch using the best ingredients for affluent customers, who didn't really appreciate the effort that had gone into it, as his own family would. No, the time had come for change.

The only way forward was to go it alone and run his own restaurant, he decided. This thought, dangling like a carrot, excited but also terrified him. They only rented their home at the moment, which made life easier should they need to buy a business. A move would certainly mean upheaval but then his daughters were young enough to adapt, he hoped. His dad had passed away and left Stuart some money. He was also earning a pretty good wage. But property prices down south were ridiculously high. It had always been cheaper up north but even that was expensive. Undeterred, during a late night browse of the web he had come across a run down restaurant with rooms above, near Lancaster that he could just about afford.

An online viewing with Izzy saw the couple put in an offer, which was duly accepted. It all happened so quickly after that. Stuart informed his boss of his impending departure, which Peter took badly, trying to increase his salary still further to retain him.

Mortgage arranged, survey completed, six weeks later the family moved. There was much work to do but it was truly invigorating. They were all thrilled at the prospect of the new business and what it could mean for the family, if it was successful. "What are you going to call it daddy?" asked his daughters.

"Clara & Agatha's has a certain ring, don't you

think?" he smiled.

"But that means we'll have to help out. Can we?"

It was certainly a family affair from the moment they arrived. Unpacking, decorating, buying tables and chairs. Izzy was in her element creating a charming and sophisticated dining room. Within weeks it was transformed from being the embarrassment of the street to the pride of it.

Importantly, Stuart was now able to cook for his family as he had always wanted to and took great pleasure watching them eating his various creations. They adored them and they were all looking so much better for it.

When he was busy writing an advertisement for the local newspaper, announcing the grand opening, in strolled the mayor, who proceeded to book the entire restaurant for the mayoral banquet.

"It will be a great pleasure sir," Stuart beamed.

"I like to support new ventures," replied the mayor. "And if your décor is anything to go by I am sure your food will be delicious."

This certainly focussed Stuart on compiling his menu. He had been busy making contacts with local producers but was still in the process of finalising arrangements. Well, he wouldn't need to book any advertisements for the foreseeable future, if they pulled this one off. Starters of spicy chicken noodle soup or sun-dried tomato frittata, mains of beef Wellington or vegetable hotpot and desserts of chocolate cake or fruit salad ought to make for happy customers even if they were vegetarian, he pondered. Many northern producers wanted a place on the wine list, too.

Izzy and the girls became the waitresses for this grand occasion and despite the odd broken glass and cracked plate, it was a stunning success. The profit generated that night meant that they didn't need to open for the rest of the week, which was just as well because they were exhausted.

Word spread and Clara & Agatha's soon became the place to be seen, where business people networked and slowly but surely notable locals started to dine there, too.

TA Saunders

EVERYBODY DREAMS

Everybody dreams. Every night. But people rarely remember their dreams, unless they make an effort to record the details before they slip away. Familiar themes and characters, strange settings, nightmares, recurring dreams, erotic dreams, dreams that make no sense, night terrors, and those unsettling hours when a person drifts between sleep and consciousness through a curtain of sensations and images. Yes, everybody dreams.

Apart from me. I do not, cannot dream. I have no name. I only exist in the dreams of others. Unrecognised, but always there. Take the youth who dreams he's running naked through the streets, pursued by strangers: I'm one of those strangers. Or the grandmother who dreams she's a child again, building sandcastles on a crowded beach while people look on approvingly: I'm one of the holiday-makers sitting in my deck chair. There's a young woman who loses something important, and searches frantically to find it: I'm one of the bystanders observing her increasing panic. And the middle-aged man who approaches a beautiful woman, only to see her walk away with someone else: I'm that someone else. And these are just a few of the people I visit. All around the world: men and women, young and old, famous and unknown, believers and non-believers: all living their own, beautiful, mysterious lives. And I also visit those who are dead. For the dead dream, too: deep, dark, slumbering dreams that never end.

And what of you and your dreams? The last time I was with you was some weeks ago. You were in a group of climbers, roped together, making your way up a narrow gorge, knowing you were lost but unwilling to admit it. You were cold and in need of help. Suddenly, you emerged onto a village green where, in front of a carnival tent, a group of well-dressed people were enjoying a picnic in the open air, singing, dancing, laughing. I was one of those people. I turned and waved to you, called to you to come and join us. You saw us. You were so happy.

People always want to discover the meaning of dreams. They don't have a meaning. They simply happen, like a sneeze or the call of an owl or a wisp of cloud in the sky. Oh, I know what the psychologists – Freud, Jung, and the rest – have to say about the significance of dreams and their links to the subconscious. And the early philosophers – Plato, Aristotle, Socrates – who believed in the divine origins of dreams as messages from the Gods. And the romantic novelists and poets and film-makers who call on them to illustrate something called 'fate' or 'destiny'. And the artists and musicians who claim them as vehicles of inspiration for their work. But they're wrong, all of them. Dreams have no origin, or explanation, or meaning, or relevance to anything that might happen in the past, present or future of anyone's life. They just happen. They just are. Just as I am. I live and breathe only in dreams. There, I'm busy, active, engaged in what I'm doing, surrounded by others. Dreams are my reality. Take them away and I would disappear.

But now, something is changing. I first noticed it several months ago. I watched you dreaming one night, wondering how and when I would make my entrance, waiting for myself to appear. But I didn't. Your dream began in a field of sheep and goats: I thought I might be a shepherd. From there, it moved to a football game: would I be among the spectators? Finally, you found yourself in the middle of a group of schoolchildren: I expected to be one of the boys and girls. But I was nowhere. Although I watched every scene, every second, of your dream, I played no part in it. How was that possible? And, if I wasn't in your dream, where was I?

And since then, the number of dreams has diminished rapidly. Not just yours. Everybody's. I don't know why. Every day, there are fewer. All over the world. Something is changing. Something has changed...as though an ancient, unspecified, and dreadful fear has been resurrected. It frightens me. I haven't yet ceased to be, but I feel like a person under threat. I see myself less and less. And the more I try to understand, the more confused I become. I want to find again the kind of certainty I knew before, to be aware of my actions, to recognize my exits and my entrances, but strange noises, new faces, harsh voices obscure them. I don't know who to trust, what to believe, or where to go. There are no signs or directions – or are there too many? And I'm struck by another thought. All the dreams in which I played a part. How can I now be sure of them? Did they really happen? Am I seeking to persuade myself to believe something that never really was?

What comes next? I've no idea. This time is out of joint. Yesterday, people dreamed, shared their dreams, were nourished by them, and were content. It was the natural way of things. But now you – all of you – seem to be coming to the end of your dreams, and if you no longer dream, there is no place for me. It's happening so quickly. I feel helpless. Is it just that I'm growing older? Is it my time? Will I simply vanish and never be remembered – apart, perhaps from a few myths and legends that vaguely recall the magical, blissful days when everybody dreamed? No...I promise you now that that will never happen. Together, we can be strong, strong enough to resist whatever approaches. Your dreams are not mere phantoms. They define you, they reveal you, they complete you, they are you. This has happened before, it will happen again. All that is lost will be recovered. Your dreams will return. I will return. Neither of us will disappear.

Ian Inglis

 Ian Inglis was born in Stoke-on-Trent and now lives in Newcastle upon Tyne. As Reader in Sociology and Visiting Fellow at Northumbria University, he has written several books and many articles around topics within popular culture. He is also a writer of fiction and his short stories have appeared in numerous anthologies and literary magazines, including Prole, Popshot, Litro, Sentinel Literary Quarterly, Riptide, The Frogmore Papers and Bandit Fiction. His debut collection of short stories *The Day Chuck Berry Died* is to be published in autumn 2022.

GOLDEN DAYS

The old man leaned heavily on the fence and stared over the tree tops towards the hamlet of Midmoor, hugging the hillside across the valley. His gaze shifted to the farmhouse at the top of the hill, where they'd tobogganed at breakneck speed every winter and then towards the pond at the bottom of the valley where they'd skinny dipped in the golden, sun-kissed summers. The memories didn't come rushing back to him, they'd never left him. His recollections of his time here, his childhood and his youth fifty years ago were fresh in his mind, perhaps, these days, rather distorted, embellished and wrapped in a cocoon of rose coloured nostalgia but they were never far below his subconscious.

He hadn't returned to recapture the heady days of his childhood or to revel in the freedom and innocence of a time of fun and laughter; he just wanted to see what had become of the place in the intervening decades. Apart from the pylons and the mobile phone mast rising high above the valley, little seemed to have changed. He could still see the school house and the white markings in the playground and the old oak tree proud as ever in the centre of the adjoining field, now sporting a coating of autumnal gold and browns. He recalled, with a grin how Tommy Brownlow had fallen out of the oak tree and broken his fall by landing on top of Archie Williams and the scrumping raids on old man Wyndham's orchard, the cricket in summer and the soccer in winter and the first kiss with Nell Perkins and the inhaled puff of his first woodbine behind the King's Head. Heady, carefree days, which he recaptured with a startling degree of clarity, wrapped in a whimsical nostalgia.

It had all ended with a brutal abruptness and unfair cruelty. His father, a giant of a man in his mid-forties dropped dead with heart failure; his mother soon remarried and the lad rapidly became unwanted. It was the beginning of a downward spiral of never-ending misfortune. He recalled how he was despatched to live with his grandmother and now he glanced over his shoulder to the bus stop where he'd waited in the rain, his pathetic bundle of possessions under his arm. She had initially rejected him but when he started work, she lavished fake attention on him whilst she relieved him of most of his meagre pay. To his disappointment he slowly realised that his friendship with the lads of Midmoor had ended. His numerous attempts to maintain a correspondence with his old school chums in the village became sporadic and in a short time, faded to nothing. He felt like he had been excluded from an exclusive club, blackballed and ostracised. He took the rejection as a personal affront, a great injustice.

It was with a certain amount of relief when his call up papers arrived and he readily disappeared into an anonymous, faceless sea of khaki. He learned fast and mastered the intricacies of foot-drill, weapons training and ironing and managed to avoid the attention of the seemingly sadistic corporals. He found a strange solace and comradeship within the ranks, an affinity similar to his memories of his idyllic, early upbringing. He was selected for training as a radio operator and showed an early flair for the trade; he worked hard and achieved good reports. On graduation he was posted to a large radio station in Germany. His embarkation leave was spent in a soldier's hostel near his barracks; it seems that he had been forgotten by his school friends.

On a wet and miserable afternoon, when he had grown tired of the hostel, he had travelled the few miles to Midmoor to see what he might find. He had alighted from the bus beside the old tavern, turned up the collar of his greatcoat against the rain and wandered along the row of low stone cottages. Old Mrs Simpson had given him a curious stare as they passed but she hurried on, without a word. He waited beside the pub; hands thrust deeply into his pockets and was rather relieved when the next bus arrived to take him back to the warmth of the hostel. As the bus crawled up the hill, he wondered why he had made the effort to return and if he would ever see the place again. And so he disappeared into the great military machine, turning his back on what remained of his family and the friends and the villagers of Midmoor. Letters from his grandmother went unanswered and letters from his mother, unopened. He spent his leisure time on the sports field and his leave exploring the great German hinterland; unbeknown to his comrades, he signed on for an extra three years and made the transition from conscript to regular. In military ideology it was a rejection of civilian life and a commitment to a long service career. It was seen by many to be a desperate attempt to immerse into an organisation, which made all the decisions and provided the soldier's every need. Had he been confronted, he would have conceded this was his reasoning for opting for such a career and that the military might treat him with greater consideration than his family and friends.

He attended training courses, put all his effort into the subject matter, passed with good grades and was rewarded with a stripe, his own room and the entitlement to a place in the Corporals' mess. It may not have been as salubrious as a Pall Mall gentlemen's club but his new position carried a degree of privilege and benefits that was not lost on him. He was to spend the next thirty-five years as a soldier, he fought in three campaigns and toured the world and was eventually promoted to

Captain. He might have recalled some of the places he'd visited or some of those he'd served with but for now, at least, he gazed at the golden hues of the valley and fancied he could hear the distant echoes of laughter of young lads at play.

He was shaken from his reverie when a voice behind him asked, "Excuse me, are you Jack Butler?"

He turned and saw a young woman, dressed in jeans and sweater.

"Aye," he answered with bewilderment. "How did you know?"

"My father was sitting at the window and saw you get off the bus. He said, 'that's Jack Butler, I'd know that frame anywhere'."

"Your father. Who is your father?"

"Tom Brownlow, he's there, by the window." She pointed to the cottage. "He's confined to a wheelchair these days and doesn't get out much. He says you were at school together. Will you come in and have a cup of tea? He says he hasn't seen or heard of you in forty years. He'll be ever so pleased to see you again and catch up. Do come."

A smile, then a grin spread across his face, as it should, to a man being shown the open door to long lost friendship.

Dan Boylan

FRENCH LEAVE

There's more than one way to kill a cat...

The holiday didn't get off to the best of beginnings. Rick had promised to be home by mid-afternoon to allow time to load the van and drive to Portsmouth. He rang at 4 o'clock to say he was stuck in traffic on the A3 and didn't know when he'd arrive. Lucy could hear country and western music in the background and knew he was really at his mother's.

When he finally did arrive home, he had a scowl chiselled on his face. "I don't wanna go France," he announced, "and my Mum ain't well."

"I know you don't wanna go to France, you've made that quite clear Rick but you are going," she told him. "Your mum will survive her latest ailment and we will have a good time. We, that is, the girls and I are tired of Bognor and you sloping off to the pub to watch football every night. So, we are all going to France to stay in a cottage near the sea for a change. Whether you enjoy it or not, depends on you. Now, load all this stuff in the van and head for Pompey."

The ferry was delayed and they landed in Caen

at 2am. "We can sleep in the van or drive through the night," she told him. His scowl deepened and he groaned, so she punched the coordinates into his sat-nav and said, "Get going, then, Mr Grumpy!"

The girls slept in the back and Lucy dozed as they sped across the French countryside. As dawn broke, he drove along a rutted dirt track and came to an abrupt halt. He elbowed her in the ribs and as she stirred, he pointed forwards and asked, "Is that it? Is that your French paradise?"

She stared through the semi-light at the row of cottages and grinned. Just as Molly had described, 'a row of white, single-storey cottages, wedged between the forest and the sand dunes. Two rooms, stone floors, simple and unmodernised, key under the door mat'.
Perfect.

He stepped inside, did a quick inspection and tutted, "Where's the bathroom?" he demanded.

"Across the yard." she replied.

"Kitchen?" he snarled.

"Whenever did you concern yourself about kitchens?" she quipped.

"It's cold and damp and it stinks!"

"It's not been used for ages, it'll be alright when it's aired. Get the van unloaded, I'll get the kettle on."

She knew that she had to cut him some slack, make some allowances for the change of holiday venue.

"Get in the back bedroom and get some sleep," she suggested. "I'll take the girls and go exploring for the day."

"Where's the pub?" he asked.

"In the village, across the estuary, you can get there on the causeway at low tide. Go to bed!"

As the sun soared, they strolled slowly around the cottages, along the edge of the forest, over the dunes and down to the beach.

"Where is everyone, Mum?" asked Ruby.

"There might be some others here later but for now, there's just us. It's good, isn't it?"

"Can we go to the village?" asked Maisie.

"When the tide goes out and you can see the causeway, then we'll walk across to the shops."

"What's the causeway?" they asked in unison.

"You'll see. Now, we're going to walk down to the water's edge, then round the point to look at the estuary. Keep your sun hats and T-shirts on. It's going to be hot."

They sat on a rock and stared across the river at the village.

"You can see the footpath going across to the village, when the water runs out to sea, then we'll walk across."

"Can we go now?" asked Maisie.

"We'll get our legs wet," said Lucy.

"Oh, let's go now, Mum," they pleaded.

They waded across the bay and as the waters swirled around their legs, they giggled. As it washed their thighs, they hooted and as it reached their waists they thought it was simply hilarious.

As they stepped onto the beach, they wrung their wet clothing and began a tour of the village and filled their basket with fresh food. Lucy spoke to the shopkeepers in French.

"When did you learn to speak French, Mum?" asked Ruby with an edge of amazement.

"At school, you will too, when you're eleven."

"The man in the butcher's shop called me 'mamsell'," said Ruby.

"It means young lady."

"Cool!" She replied.

They sat on the beach and ate fresh bread, cheese and grapes, then paddled in the rock pools until Lucy said, "Time to go back."

Rick was sitting on the front step, glum and long faced. He watched them wade through the shallow water without interest. He didn't rise or come to meet them and stayed mute when Maisie declared, "We crossed the river and got our clothes wet Dad."

"Is there a pub?" he asked gloomily.

Lucy knew what was coming. "Go play at the water's edge girls, see if you can find some shells."

"I'll tell you now," she said, "there is a pub but there's no TV."

He groaned, "Why have you done this to me?"

"You don't die from lack of football or beer, Rick. You've a family who have no interest in pubs or soccer. But I'll tell you what I'll do, I'll meet you half-way, Bognor one year, France the next."

"They can play all day on the beach in Bognor, what's wrong with watching football and having a pint?" he protested.

"Bognor one year, France the next," she repeated.
"So there's no pub here, no English, no blokes and no football. Happy holiday," he snapped.

"You're a family man now, not a teenager, not a soccer groupie, Rick. You spend a third of your life in the van, a third in the pub and a third sleeping. Two weeks, that's all, just be a father for two weeks! Then you can go back to do what you do best, watching football."

"I look after my kids," he snapped, "I do more than my share, I do loads more than other blokes."

She was quiet for a second and he relaxed, "Who is Lambert and Bale?" she asked.

"They're footballers, why?"

"And who is Tracey?"

"An old girlfriend, why?"

"It's just that you talk of them in your sleep," she lied. "You never mention my name, or the girls!"

He blushed and his jaw moved up and down but nothing came out. "And you were at your mum's when you rang yesterday, not stuck in traffic, weren't you?!"
He lowered his head. "You sent your mum a birthday card but forgot the girl's birthdays and mine," she slipped in, neatly.

"I.....I..," he stammered. But she had an arsenal

of 'guilt ammunition' and she was banging them in the back of the net as fast as he pulled them out. "You see, when we go to Bognor, you invite your mum and then your mates turn up and the girls and I get relegated to baggage class. We have to work our days and evenings around you, your mum and football. When the girls turn in and you're at the pub, I get to spend the evening watching TV. Well, not this year Rick, this year we're having a family holiday far away from it all!"

He sat, head in hands, beaten and dejected. The minutes ticked by. She looked down to the girls at the water's edge as he slowly came to terms with it all. He took a deep breath.

"Okay", he conceded, "Okay! France one year, Bognor the next. Is there any beer and what's for dinner?"

"One, nil," thought Lucy.

Dan Boylan

Dan Boylan is a retired Yorkshireman, living in Wickham, Hampshire. He has been writing articles and travel features for a series of magazines and other publications for 25 years. "My favourite genre is short fiction which is liberally sprinkled with intrigue and the unexpected, often with humour and a twist in the tail/tale! I create imaginative story baselines with colourful character profiles and intriguing plots." Dan has been a member of various writers' groups for quarter of a century producing more than 60 short stories, dramas and rattling good yarns. "My daughter claims that I am an absolute mine of useless information," smiles Dan.

MY DIARY

entry for May 12, 2021

I have somehow managed to make it to my 70th year, still married and still living on the east coast of Scotland.When I say living, I use the term loosely. Perhaps treading water or hanging on would be more accurate.

For someone who has been accustomed to travelling the world from childhood, being confined to barracks these past few months has been particularly difficult. The furthest I get these days is taking the dog for his daily walk along a disused railway track.

Adjusting to retirement was hard enough and then Covid came along and put that crisis in the shade.

With five months of 2021 already spent, the easing of lockdown feels as though this year is finally getting started.

The rejoining of life's procession again for me is tentative, one of caution and replete with trepidation, nevermind the loss of social confidence. My optimism severely dented, replaced by the dread of the other shoe dropping by way of a new, more pernicious variant or another surge of infection, tramples any green shoots of hope.

I remain skeptical when I see this virus rampaging around the world that we can afford to risk returning to a world of close contact and freedom of movement. In many ways the way we had conducted our lives before may have changed forever.

I try as a consequence to seek consolation in the smaller more tangible gifts in life. Today the sun is shining, I can sit outside and have my breakfast and hear just birdsong with my canine companion at my feet. The simplest pleasures of life being realised.

I am also free from any physical pain or overt mental anguish so far.

The future, although far from certain, has to be taken on a day-to-day basis. There are many who sadly are a lot worse off than I. I should learn to be more thankful.

The aspirations of resuming travel, being more gregarious, daring and adventurous again may well be over now for me.

It is difficult to contemplate a worthwhile future right now with so much mortality and increasing hardship, greed and inequality occurring around the world.

I am recording this today, May 12, 2021 as

another day spent waiting like Godot for a brighter and more certain future. I know that deep down this will not come to pass in my life time but I hope that my genetic torchbearers will see better days ahead.

Roger Knight

THE KIHIKIHI
HOTEL

"I stood out in the open cold to see the essence of the eclipse which was its perfect darkness.
I stood in the cold on the porch and could not think of anything so perfect as man's hope of light in the face of darkness."

Richard Eberhart

I still like to relive those moments when I had my celebratory beer in the Kihikihi Hotel, after passing my state final exam becoming qualified as a New Zealand State Registered Psychiatric nurse.

"Free at last, free at last, thank God Almighty I'm free at last," was the Martin Luther King refrain I said to myself, realising that my self-imposed exile of four years was over, the world was now at my feet.

Carried on a tide of triumph, I felt I was on my way to conquering the world, that it was now my oyster. I could travel to my choice of destination and become the master of my own destiny.

That all pervading sense of freedom was euphoric, heightened by a sense of accomplishment and achievement at finally crossing the finish line.

Having reached the end of my working life, I still reflect on that celebratory beer, remembering what it felt like to be free, replete with optimism and ambition.

It was one of life's summit experiences that never leaves me.

Roger Knight

 Roger Knight lives in St Andrews, Fife. Since retiring, he has been writing about aspects of his life story that he hope readers might find of interest and perhaps challenge their assumptions about this world. Having spent the first part of his life in Bermuda and Jamaica and then latterly in Australasia and the Middle East, he is fortunate enough to have a varied number of experiences and material to draw on. His genre of expression tends to be: memoir in a short story/prose form as well as essay writing. Roger is a regular contributor to the *Writer and Readers* magazine and has had several short stories published in various anthologies.

YELLOW

The warplane passed low enough to shake the remains of the apartment block. Dust dribbled from amputated beams and exposed steel.

Anton let go of the JCB's controls for just an instant, fearing the remaining walls would fall. The North side was half gone already, but the other three, unstable, towered over him, their glassless windows portals to an unforgiving sky.

His shoulder tightened from the week-old bullet wound but he welcomed the spasms as reminders that he was alive, not done for yet. Even now, digging through rubble instead of wielding a gun, he had purpose.

Would Yulia think less of him, he wondered, if she knew his situation? An enemy gunman had cut short his heroics and left him with no option but to help recover bodies from rubble.

Would she no longer see him as the brave upstart from that night in the bar, when he defended her from drunken thugs?

When the police arrived at the scene Anton had finished his drink too fast - and threw up on Yulia's feet. She didn't move. "My hero," she quipped as they cuffed him. When Anton emerged from jail the next morning he'd found Yulia sitting outside with a flask of hot coffee and an offer to buy him breakfast.

Instant love.

Yulia was an amazing woman, a strong, self assured heroine, who in truth had been his salvation, lifted him from drunken loneliness. He could never have predicted he'd one day marry this lady and plan to adopt a child with her.

Yulia had insisted they would rehome a beautiful girl, dress her in the brightest yellows and make her a princess that would light up the world. Anton loved the plan, but never did he expect such darkness.

Now he checked his phone. Each day for a few minutes, a single bar would appear, and a smattering of communication was possible.

Messages would arrive by the dozen from queues of millions and then the signal was lost again. Anton heard talk of picture messages and voicemails in the early days. None for him so far.

Instead he used his mind to picture Yulia in that last moment he'd spent with her, before a panicked crowd swallowed her up, and her train departed with many running alongside it.

Above Anton, bricks and cables now fell away from the surrounding walls as something rumbled beneath. Men shouted orders to move back, their uniformed presences scattering outward.

Cables dangled near to the JCB, occasionally

teasing with sparks - the death throes of a dwindling electricity supply. Anton had become accustomed to this.

Something hissed.

One of the men shouted: "Gas leak! Everybody out!"

But Anton's mind was elsewhere.

"Hey, you in the digger! Move!"

Near the centre of the wreckage a jet of dust shot upward. Anton realised the gas main had been punctured. His phone beeped as he moved to exit the JCB. He paused, his hand resting upon the door handle. He postponed reality. Gas must wait. An actual message had arrived. Please God, let it be her. Please God.

His eyes widened when he saw the image. Yulia had made it. She had crossed the border. Against all the odds, his wife was safe. Not one hair was out of place. Not one scratch on her perfect face.

In her selfie Yulia sat proud and defiant in her wheelchair. Her smile uplifted his spirits, just as it did outside the jail that morning. "Waiting for you", read her simple caption.

Anton ran a finger over the cracked screen. "We still have our plan."

Sparks crackled. Gas ignited. A fireball exploded around him.

The blast toppled two of the walls, knocked the JCB on its side, sent it tumbling with Anton inside, a bean in a can, slammed his body as it rolled. Finally it came to rest against a car whose front end was buried in rubble.

Fragments of nearby conversation bounced around Anton's head.

"We can't search here any more. The fire's too dangerous."

"We can't just leave them… There might even be -"

"Forget it. They should have evacuated. There'll be another site that needs us."

"What about that guy in the JCB?"

"He was already wounded. No chance he survived that. We can't stay."

The dialog was muffled then eventually faded, leaving only their vanishing footsteps.

A roar in the sky approached from the East. Another plane, come to finish the job on a new fiery target. They'd be aiming to wipe out the recovery team themselves.

Urgency gripped Anton. He fought to control his breathing, to regain focus. He pulled himself out of the wrecked machine and fell to the ground.

Then he heard it, a mesmerising sound from inside the half-buried car. The cry punctured the volume of nearby flames, approaching jet engines and of collapsing walls. It pained him more than his wounds, pierced his very heart, yet fuelled him with hope: It was the sound of a crying baby.

Anton got up and staggered round the vehicle, peered inside and saw upon the front seats the bodies of a young couple slumped against each other, blocks of concrete bearing down on their torsos.

How had the team missed this? So focused on the fallen apartments they didn't check the perimeter for vehicles.

That sound. Of God, that sound.

The back doors were locked. Anton kicked in a rear passenger window and peered inside. And there she was: a baby girl wrapped in a bright yellow blanket. The infant locked eyes with Anton, stopped crying and gurgled happily, as if overjoyed to see someone. Anton, in spite of himself, smiled.

He knew he'd found a princess who would light up the world.

He gathered the child up in his arms, still wrapped in her bright yellow blanket, and started running.

Owen Southwood

 Owen has been writing creative fiction since childhood. Born in 1974, he grew up in Suffolk, England where he now lives with his wife and two children. Owen works in IT and writes short fiction for fun and to provoke thought. He writes in a variety of genres and topics. Some of his short stories have been published but Owen dreams of publication as a novelist. He has written two unpublished novels and is working on a third. Owen follows politics and wishes for a free, open and united world.

GIFT

When Curse opened his eyes he saw a system and a system can be manipulated for your own personal gain. He saw people scurrying around in fields. He saw that they manipulated the system and therefore were inherently bad. When Gift opened her eyes she saw the world and the world was good. She saw the people and saw that they were selfless and kind hearted and were therefore good. Then they saw each other. Curse saw Gift was good. Gift saw that Curse was evil and therefore a threat.

Curse moved first, striking a savage blow that met a wall of flesh and released a burst of energy. Gift swung back but Curse simply mimicked her and her fist met a mountain-like body. Gift swung again and Curse dodged.

"Aah I'm fast," Curse thought. "I wonder how fast?" Curse flickered and appeared in front of Gift. He swung, but she was no longer there.

"You're fast but I'm faster," Gift said from behind him.

Curse lashed out but once again Gift was no longer there and his fist met nothing but air. Gift tutted from Curse's left and he lashed out with his foot catching Gift in the stomach, throwing her back. It seemed that they were at an impasse. They circled each other, each looking for an opening. Then circles of energy burst from their bodies. They simultaneously swung their fists only to catch each other, in the face, in complete sync. This caused an explosion of energy that spat them both out like comets hurtling towards the earth, to crash into the same building, rich in grandeur and size.

When Gift opened her eyes the last thing she remembered was the explosion, her ears still rung and bright spots tap danced across her vision. When her vision finally cleared she saw the handsome but worried face of a strapping young man. Behind him, almost eclipsed by his immense body was a hole through which she must have crashed, into the room in which she now lay. The room was filled with wooden counters. From the ceiling hung great metal hooks from which hung gargantuan slabs of meat. She then took notice of where she lay. It appeared that she had smashed into one of the wooden counters. She shifted and felt something poke her back. She rummaged beneath her and pulled out a small, metal pronged item.

"Are you okay, Ma'am?" asked the muscular young man.

Gift held up the metal pronged thing, questioningly.

"It's a fork, Ma'am," said the young man.

Gift looked puzzled.

"You use it to eat, Ma'am."

This seemed to satisfy Gift. She then turned her attention to herself. It seemed whilst she was unconscious she had been bandaged.

"You helped me, why?" she asked, speaking finally.

"It was the right thing to do, Ma'am," he said.

"Then I shall reward you," she said.

"No thank you, Ma'am, I simply did what any person would do," he said shaking his head.

"In which case you just made up my mind. You are pure hearted, therefore your reward shall be great."

She focused her mind on her hand and a ball of light formed in it.

"Take my hand and become the Champion of Light, the Portrayer of Good."

At first he was hesitant but then he grasped her hand and was engulfed in a blinding light. For the time being his consciousness faded.

"When you awake you shall be born anew. Your strength shall be great. No man or woman, if there be the slightest bit of corruption in their hearts, shall harm you. You shall go forth and vanquish evil."

Curse opened his eyes, his vision eclipsed by an angry yet beautiful face hovering above him. He moved the sheets of the bed in which he lay, in a grand bedroom. He looked down at himself and saw that he was bandaged. He looked at the face again and read it like a book.

"You are wondering whether or not I can pay for the damage to your home."

"Yes," said the owner of the face, obviously a woman.

"You see the world as a system to be manipulated for your own gain."

"Yes," she said, a spark of recognition flashed in her eyes.

"Then here is your payment."

Curse held out his hand. She took it cautiously and was immediately engulfed by every shadow in the room. She dropped to the ground writhing in agony, the pain making her black out.

"When you rise you shall be invincible, my Champion of Evil. You will be able to pass on your power to others so that they may serve you. Then you shall go forth and extinguish good."

Thus the battle for good and evil started anew.

When the young man woke, he saw that the beautiful stranger, that had crashed into his life, was once again unconscious. He realised that he felt powerful. On top of that he could sense evil and track it, so he did. Eventually he came to the master bedroom and beheld a being enrobed in bandages, laying on the bed. This must be the evil his mistress sent him to vanquish. He leapt into the bed effortlessly, picked Curse up with one hand and snapped his neck, killing him. Then he spied his old mistress, the owner of the house, and picked her up with care, though he knew that she was now a creature of Curse. He walked over to the window and looked out, the building was set on a cliff making them thousands of feet above the ground. He was remorseful about what he had to do but knew that whilst she lived so did evil and he threw her to her death.

Kato Smart

 Nineteen year old Kato has autism and ADHD. He enjoys Trading Card Games: Yu-Gi-Oh, Magic the Gathering and Pokemon. Kato has a vast Lego collection, enjoys watching Marvel movies and creating role play scenarios. He is busy writing a novel, *Conflict, Book 1* in the Good v Evil series.

THE SOUND
OF THE BELL

The day had been full of bustle and petulant rain. AJ's default setting was to blob in front of the television and eat take away comfort food, maybe even ice-cream.

But a part of her being suggested something else, something radical.

She was an irregular member of a Buddhist group that met weekly to practice silent meditation together and listen to a teaching - real or lifted from one of the many internet libraries. This had converted to Zoom meetings sometime during the Covid crisis and AJ had lost the habit to attend, through antipathy and apathy. Not totally true, she had joined in, once or twice.

In a deep oceanic part of her being, she remembered the words 'wise mind', being used to describe this neglected self and the voice became louder. "You could join in tonight, see what you think..." and therein was the problem. The week had been all about thinking.

The old email with the link to the group was found and it worked. The wi-fi miraculously connected and a black square called 'host' let her in at once. The small talk seemed to be done and each square, some with real faces, some with photoshopped, definitely aspirational backgrounds and some called Trevor's tablet or iPhone II, were checking in, responding to the question: "How are you travelling?"

Oh God; no idea..... dilemma - do I turn on my camera? Have I wiped my the tomato sauce from my face? Combed my hair? Overhead light or lamp? Unusually, I couldn't wait for the meditation to start. I yearned for the cessation of sounds - others' voices; the background barking of dogs, no doubt seeking inner peace and with only flickering hope, my own reticulating waterfall of thoughts.

Then it dripped into my head, the voice of tonight's teacher, suggesting we might watch the thoughts that arise and begin to view them as either helpful in achieving a settled and spacious mind - definitely my goal or unhelpful in that they distract and seduce us away from that place.

I soon caught myself wondering and then worrying about tomorrow. Would I get a good and restful night's sleep? Would I know how to handle the tricky client I could anticipate and then the ones I couldn't...could I be ... what did they want... should I say...?

And then I asked myself, "Is this thinking helping

you slow down, let go or is it adding more to the rock pile of your mind?

But then the questions faded and I found myself visualising a shepherd, snoozing lazily in the shade of a tree, his resting, unstraying sheep in the foreground. Obedient and somnolent. The scene was bucolic and technicolour in the best classical pastoral tradition; it could have been enclosed in a gilt frame and hung with the lesser works section of a gallery.....

"Helpful or unhelpful? Staying with spacious or racing away with embellishment, a story..."

And then the bold intrusion of the meditation bell into this unusual yet very pleasurable experience. Generally AJ was as restless as a bag of weasels, fidgety, looking at the clock....

And the question was being asked, again... "How are you travelling?"

She felt hope and was able to say, "Just breathing..." and that was enough.

Patricia McLoughlin

Patricia McLoughlin was born in Sydney, Australia. She attended Sydney University and was involved in the student drama society. She is a Grief and Bereavement Counsellor in Sydney and a beginner baby meditator, Buddhist and writer.

PROTECTING
LITERATURE

Kateryna waited until daylight. The only time she could venture outside. There is a curfew at night. The city has been under martial law for over a week. A week ago, the Russians had surrounded the city and the constant bombardment had become part of her everyday life.

This morning the sirens are muted as Kateryna picks her way through the rubble; the remains of a library. She has acquired an abandoned shopping trolley, left in the stairwell of her apartment block. She remembers wiping the blood off the handle.

The air is tainted. She tastes sulphur on her tongue. It is hard to tell if it is the smoke leftover from the night of shelling or thick cloud; maybe it is both. It seems darker today.

The trolley is almost full of books. Kateryna picks them out from the bricks and the twisted iron beams. Dogs bark somewhere in the distance and three people pass her by in a hurry, carrying loads on their backs. They do not acknowledge her and she is grateful. She has never been one for idle chat, not even before the invasion.

Kateryna only collects novels - works of fiction. She has always been a book hoarder. She takes advantage of the situation. She did feel guilty at first but she told herself this is her contribution. Preserving the library. She would return them once the war ends. Or would she? She is not sure.

I might be dead soon anyway.

The trolley full, she manoeuvres down the road, zigzagging between smouldering craters and burning cars. The pavements are far too hazardous to move on. Bombed-out buildings lean awkwardly and dangerously over her, forcing her to keep in the centre of the street. A clapped-out Skoda passes by, coughing and spluttering. Five or six young men squeezed into the vehicle carry machine guns and head towards the city's outskirts to defend what remains. She prays for their safety and wonders about joining the militia again but she knows they wouldn't want her.

Kateryna was born with missing fingers on her right hand and a clubfoot that hinders her movement. She would do her bit by saving as much of the library as possible.

Thankfully, the elevators in her apartment block still work and she pushes the overloaded trolley out into the corridor, towards her apartment. She does not bother to lock her door; it is easier for her to leave it ajar. Then the sirens begin to sound out again, like a whaling child. She hurries into the marginal safety of her flat.

Already the hallway is lined from the floor to the ceiling with books and she can only just squeeze the trolley down the aisle. Once into her studio apartment, she looks around the room. The single, unmade bed reveals the stack of books stored underneath. Empty tins of meatballs with spoons still in them sit on the kitchen counter, nestled on more books. She has almost run out of room. The walls are lined with Zabuzhko, Zhadan, Matios, Kostenko and even translated works by Dickens, Trollope, and Orwell.

Looking lost on where to place her latest collection, suddenly the ground shakes with a massive explosion. Dust comes raining down from the ceiling, and she hits the floor, covering her head. There is the distant rattle of gunfire and another explosion. She sees the window bow from the blast. Quickly she rises and begins to stack the books from the trolley in front of the window, almost shut off from the outside world. Working at speed, she gathers more books from the hallway and stacks them up until the light no longer comes in.

Kateryna sits in the darkened room; a single candle lights up an area of her bed and she reads Anna Karenina in the dim light as the bombs fall around her. She blocks it out, her mind in Tolstoy's world. Another colossal blast shakes the room; the candle flickers and dies. The window smashes behind the book wall. She holds her breath for what seems like hours. The shelling eventually ceases, and the sirens sleep.

The next day, Kateryna begins collecting every book she can find.

She will fill every apartment, every house that still stands, and when peace returns, she hopes and dreams of building a new library - a bigger and better one than before.

MJ White

 MJ White was born in Southampton in 1975 and is frankly amazed to be still alive today. He struggled at school; dyslexia and immaturity played their part. After leaving school, he spent far too much time dancing to rave music in the fields. Eventually, he fell into the catering industry and worked as a chef, a private security guard and a drug worker. He hung up his chef's knives in 2017 and returned to full-time education and is currently final degree year studying Creative Writing at the University of Winchester. He likes writing in all genres. However, speculative/ realism/horror/dystopia and apocalyptic fiction are where his writing tends to lead him. MJ White's debut novel *Faze (The City of Addicts)* was released in August 2021.

VISION OF PEACE

Chained, blindfolded and stripped of all human dignity, the prisoner sits on a cold concrete floor. The airless room echoes the cries and screams of the other prisoners. How often had he prayed to God? He had at least enough faith to know that one day he would be free. Free to feel and smell the green grass beneath his feet, the sun beaming down on him, feel the touch of rain on his face. Oh how he longed for freedom.

Hearing the guards' heavy footsteps, the prisoner puts his head down. He had learned his lesson from day one not to glance at his captors. They had as much regard for him as they had for an insect as they stamped on his body and kicked at his head.

He was kept in total isolation. Days had turned into months but to the prisoner it felt like an eternity. He played mind games to keep his brain active. At least he had got plenty of time to meditate, he thought. And then he realized that he must still have retained a glimmer of his sense of humour, if that was possible in the hell of the rat hole he was in. That is exactly what he felt like - a rat, trapped in a man-made hell-hole. The guard put his food down beside him and took off his chains. They usually allowed him just five minutes to eat his food and stretch his emaciated body before they put the chains back on. This time when they came back, the chains were not put back on, nor the blindfold. What's more he had company. Two more prisoners had joined him. He had been on his own for so long, lost in his own thoughts and dreams. At first, he enjoyed the company, except for when he wanted to sleep or just to be at peace with himself. They would talk constantly. Why were they here? They did not know either. Like him, they had not done anything wrong but that, apparently, was not the issue. Their captors were trying to make a point and the prisoners were innocent victims of terrorists.

The prisoner looked at his new cellmates, one young, one old. He thought of their families, as his thoughts were never far away from his own. Would he ever see them again? Hope, faith, having a balanced nature and his bible kept him sane. In fact the bible was the only thing that they never took from him. He had read every word of the good book. His body was weak but his spirit was stronger than ever. The prisoner sang hymns and told jokes; anything to keep the other two prisoners' spirits up.

Sometimes, late at night after the wailing, muffled sobbing and manic laughter from the other cells had died down, the prisoner would lie awake, relieved to be able at last be at peace with his thoughts. If there is a hell, he thought, he was living it. Would he go mad like the others? Maybe he was already mad, for after his cell mates had talked themselves to sleep, a round ball of golden light would appear before him. A vision with the aura of an angel would step out of the light, comforting him and giving him answers to all his many questions.

He eventually realized that he wasn't crazy and he came to believe that he would soon be able to fight against prejudice and the ignorance of society towards injustice, for freedom of the innocent who were locked in cells like himself. He knew that there was only one God, yet people were fighting in his name. Why, when God asked people to be kind to each other and not use religion as an excuse in his name, to maim, murder and torture? The world was facing a spiritual millennium and the guards were totally unaware that the prisoner they had been torturing was to be the saviour, who would at last bring peace to the world.

Like Jesus Christ, before him, the prisoner would forgive them.

Sheila Barker

Sheila enjoys her family life but also enjoys meeting new people and is passionate about animals, all creatures including spiders. For many

 years she belonged to a writer's group. "I have just finished writing my second book, one of a series that leads towards the mystic and supernatural," she reveals. The first, *Palms of Destiny* has been published. Some of her short stories have been published and broadcasted on radio. I believe the actions and the paths we take not only influence ourselves but all life forms and that is why I would never kill a spider," she says.

THE RELUCTANT RECLUSE

The last thing Lawrence Gillman expected to be doing on a stormy Saturday night was trudging through a swampy estate in the middle of Dartmoor. He pulled the collar up on his coat, not that it protected him against the howling wind and lashing rain, and pushed forward towards the dim light in the window of the grand house.

He pressed the glowing button of the doorbell but instead of a chime, a voice came over an intercom.

"Yes?"

"Lawrence Gillman, from the *Okehampton Echo*."

A buzzer sounded and Lawrence pushed the door into a vast entrance hall, which was in complete darkness. In the flash of the lightning, he could see staircases running up either side of the hall, meeting at a balcony above a large doorway. Off to the left he could see a light shining through a half open doorway, the rustling of papers, could be heard from within.

"Mr Van Wyse?" asked Lawrence, pushing the door fully open. Inside the drawing room sat a lone figure in a high-backed chair, close enough to the fire to warm the occupant but not to scorch the leather of the chair.

"Mr Van Wyse?"

The figure was still unmoving, his profile flickering in the glow of the fire.

"You requested I visit you."

"I do not like visitors," replied a hushed voice. "There have been no visitors here for twenty-six years, except for my grocery deliveries."

"I understand you are reclusive, Mr Van Wyse. The most famous since Howard Hughes, it is said."

"I requested your visit to confess to you, Mr Gillman."

"Confess?"

"You have received some letters from the killer of one of your journalistic brethren, who has taunted you for almost a month... I am that man."

The tension Lawrence had felt melted away. He gave a chuckle as he took the matching chair across from the reclusive man.

"Why do you lie to me, Mr Van Wyse?"

"You assume I lie?"

"You've been locked away in this house since you lost your mother and father in a car accident. You didn't leave your house and you expect me to believe you committed a murder?"

"You are correct, I have not left my house for over forty years; since the day my mother and father died."

Lawrence removed a tattered notebook from his pocket, opened to a fresh page and clicked the top of his pen dramatically.

"I'm all ears," he said, sarcastically waving his pen over the notebook. "Tell me how someone who hasn't left their home for so long could possibly commit a murder?"

Magnus Van Wyse took his eyes from the roaring fire for the first time and looked Lawrence straight in the eyes.

"Would you consider yourself an adequate reporter, Mr Gillman?"

Lawrence was somewhat thrown by the question.

"I'm more than adequate. Do you know I've been offered jobs at *The Daily Telegraph* and *The Times*?"

"I was aware of those offers, as I am also aware that you have not accepted either. Is there a justifiable reason you have not taken those positions? I am sure they would provide a better living than the *Okehampton Echo* has to offer."

"Where I choose to work is no concern of yours."

Lawrence had had enough of these games. Sighing, he rose to leave.

"You are walking away from a murderer giving you an exclusive confession?"

"I'm walking away from a man who has been alone for far too long."

As Lawrence strode towards the door, he

stopped short when the hushed voice from before boomed out across the drawing room, "You killed Brian Peters!"

He turned back to find Magnus walking towards him, some letters in his outstretched hand. "You wrote the letters to yourself. I have examined every news article you have ever written and there are distinct patterns within your writing, Mr Gillman."

"Let's say I wrote the letters, as a way to get myself recognised; a name on a big newspaper. That doesn't prove I killed anyone."

"There are too many details in the letters that only the true killer would know. There is no doubt that you killed him."

There was a change in the reporter's demeanour. He had begun to swagger and a broad grin spread across his face.

"Prove it," he said, slapping himself on the chest. "Prove I killed him."

"These letters are all the proof I need. Once I take my suspicions to the police they will no doubt see the connection."

The grin faded and Lawrence advanced on the older man with an air of menace.

"Give me those letters and you won't get hurt."

"I am afraid these letters will be in the hands of the police by morning and you will be under arrest."

"I already killed Brian. You really think I won't kill you?"

"Sounds like a confession to me," came a voice from behind Lawrence.

He turned to find a broad-shouldered man standing in the doorway to the entrance hall.

"Inspector Lansdown, you obviously heard everything?"

"I did, Mr Van Wyse. Mr Gillman confessed to the murder of Brian Peters."

"I didn't confess!"

"You're under arrest for murder, Mr Gillman."

An officer appeared, removing Lawrence from the room, leaving Inspector Lansdown and Magnus alone.

"How did you know?" asked the inspector.

"Exactly how I described. His writing patterns and his unwillingness to accept my confession. Any reporter worth his salt would jump on a confession by a killer. He couldn't accept it because he already knew it wasn't me because he was guilty of the crime."

A young girl walked in with a smile on her face and a tear in her eye. This was Alla Petrushevych, the woman originally accused of the reporter's murder. Magnus spoke to her in a foreign language and placed a hand on her arm. She nodded and turned away.

"What did you say?" asked the inspector.

"I told her that no matter what happens in life, always keep hope in your heart."

TJ Waters

TJ Waters is 38 years old and was born in Portsmouth. He spent his life growing up in nearby Havant. "I've always had a big imagination from the first day I read my favourite book, *Around The World In 80 Days*. As a child I was often found inventing my own stories and it became my lifetime dream to have my own book published." He has a love of walking and is always thinking of others. "So in 2014 I combined the two by completing the South Downs Way Walk, with friends, for charity, by walking from Eastbourne to Winchester in four days."

TIM SAUNDERS
PUBLICATIONS
publishing great poetry
and short stories

Do you have a book you would like to publish?

email
tsaunderspubs@gmail.com

monthly writing prompts at:
tsaunderspubs.weebly.com

Printed in Great Britain
by Amazon